The Parlor

KEN ZAHN

First Printing

Published by
Southern Lion Books
Financial Mystery Series
1280 Westminster Way
Madison, Georgia 30650

southernlionbooks.com

Manufactured in the United States of America.

Library of Congress Control Number: 2011932177

ISBN: 978-1-935272-14-4

The paper in this book meets the guidelines for permanence
and durability of the Committee on Production Guidelines
for Book Longevity of the Council on Library Resources.

Photo Credits: J.H. Segars Collection,
Google Public Domain, University of Georgia Pandora (1934).
Cover: Exterior of Home of Jeff and Linda Albe
and Parlor of Tom and Sandra Rosseter, Eatonton, Georgia.

The Parlor

CHAPTER ONE

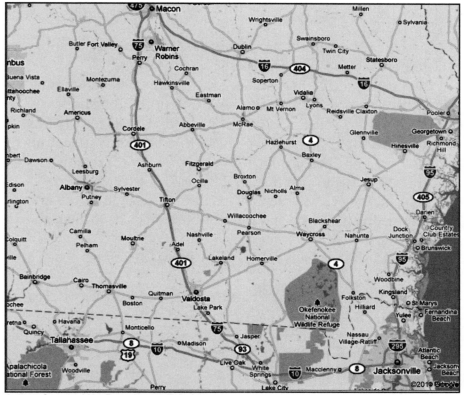

© 2011 Google, Map Data © 2011 Tele Atlas

"Arthur, there's a man on the phone who wants to talk to you." Silvia, my long-time assistant, worked just outside my office. Communication in many cases was by loud voice. Not very professional, but a very fast delivery system. In the beginning Silvia and I worked in a ten by ten office. Rarely did I close my office door even today. She and I talked to the same clients. I could hear what she said, and she knew what I said. No mystery with miscommunication and we were both up to date on my clients.

Deep in thought, I hadn't heard my phone ring. Working on a new financial plan for an old client of mine was taking my full concentration. My plan writing goes way back to pre-computer, so all plans custom fit the client. I'd been trying to retire for several years. My office staff had grown, and I'd hired other planners to handle cases for me, but every now and then an interesting problem pulled me back in.

"Arthur! Will you pick up the phone? Or do you want me to take a message? Make up your mind!" she shouted at me.

My temper got the best of me. I was within mere minutes of finishing the plan and the interruption threw me out of whack.

"Who is it?" I yelled back. Silvia's insistent tone and my frustration at being interrupted at the crucial ending point had put me on edge. All my well thought-out plan conclusions were disappearing. I quickly jotted down some finalization notes.

"Temper, temper," she replied looking me straight in the eye. My mouth wouldn't move. My brain was still thinking about the plan. She laughed and answered my question.

"A Mr. Lancaster. He is calling from a town in Georgia that I can't spell or pronounce."

"Temper, temper" hadn't cooled me down. Silvia had worked for me for years. She was considered my assistant but she also worked with me on a few financial planning cases. She was very efficient and the only one who could get away with "temper, temper."

"What does he want?" Back and forth we went. The rest of the office thought we were crazy when they heard us. Fortunately this only happened occasionally.

"He wants to hire you to do a financial plan."

"Is he a referral from a client?"

"He didn't say."

With my temper still hot, she should have asked. She knew better. Now that my train of thought had been broken, why not find out why this "Mr. Lancaster" needed me? Fortunately my thoughts were safe and the plan could be completed later.

"Hello, this is Arthur." There was no need to take out my frustration on him.

"Arthur, my name is James Johnson Lancaster. I go by "JJ". One of my University of Georgia buddies, Brett Longfellow, used you to straighten out his financial affairs. He said you were very good. I need help."

Geez, the phone was like a hot potato. The Longfellow case was a messy divorce. Drop the potato. Hang up. No, that wouldn't be very professional, let's see what he says. No more messy divorces if that's where this was going.

"My assistant said you live in Georgia. What was the town again?" Just how far was he from Tampa?

He told me the town's name and he spelled it out. Once upon a time, I'd been a salesman in rural North Florida, Georgia and Alabama, but even so, I'd never heard of this town. It had to be very rural. After a long explanation, where was it?

Before I-75 and I-95 were built in the 1960's, the only way to get to Florida from the north was to go down the many U.S. highways that ran north to south through Alabama and Georgia such as US 1, US 19, and US 41. After the interstates were built, time stopped in parts of Alabama and Georgia, especially along parts of the Alabama-Georgia state line and in a portion of eastern non-coastal Georgia. This town with an Indian name was one of those towns that got left behind.

JJ continued talking up a storm, but I needed time to think. To stall him, I told him to hold on for a moment while I got a pad of paper. Computers can be wonderful. Within seconds, the town appeared on the computer screen, the time it took to get there, and other basic information.

As I started to respond, JJ hit me between the eyes. "I thought you big city financial planners would be computer savvy. What took you so long?" He laughed. He knew what I was doing.

Geez. "How can I help you?"

"I want you to come up here and help me work out a financial transfer of my family's land and business to my sons without paying the jerks in Washington their thieving portion. Arthur, are you one of those Yankees?"

"Does that make a difference?" This guy was really irritating.

"Well, maybe. You can never tell with Florida. We should have never conceded North Florida. It should have stayed with Georgia."

This was getting silly, but for some reason I just couldn't hang up. He was a referral from a very good client. My practice had been built on referrals.

"I was born up north and moved to Florida many years ago."

"Well, that's OK; at least you didn't go to the University of Florida. Those boys did it again last season"

I'd wasted all this time, let's see his reason.

"JJ, let's get back to your reason for calling." It was do or die time. I didn't want to get sidetracked into discussing the merits of the University of Georgia's football team versus University of Florida's.

Football is big in the South. The University of Georgia versus University of Florida football game is a biggie played in Jacksonville. It's an easy hour's ride from Gainesville, but many hours from Athens, Georgia. In addition, Florida has won most of the recent games, making it a long ride home for Georgia fans.

My mind had drifted for a few moments. That was bad news for a financial planner. JJ had started into his reason for contacting me. "Pay attention, concentrate, and don't get distracted thoughts" energized my brain.

"Listen, Arthur, I have a business that consists of farmland and processing plants. The farmland can grow cotton, tobacco, or peanuts. We try to rotate it. We're even trying corn. Some of the land is dedicated to trees. We're doing basic commodity processing but our cotton clothing division closed years ago. Damn foreigners destroyed our textile manufacturing business and now the economy is affecting our cotton sales. Cotton prices have skyrocketed!"

"Bottom line - you're making too much money?"

"Yes. The corporation, my sons and I are in the top income tax brackets. Since land owners with a small amount of acreage can't compete in today's capital-sensitive market, they typically sell their land to us for bargain basement prices and we easily incorporate their land into our land use plan."

JJ was making sense. A land owner with small acreage couldn't afford the equipment to operate competitively. They could sell the land minus their homestead to JJ, buy all the material possessions Americans crave with that money, and probably continue to work for JJ in exchange for moderate income. Not a bad life, but they're spending their children's inheritance. However, the next generation, if they're smart, will get a good education and move to the larger cities in the South.

"What is your net worth? Can you give me a ballpark figure?"

"Arthur, that's my problem. I don't know. The value of the land can vary greatly depending on who you talk to. Our processing plants are old. They make money but not as much as my commodities. There aren't any decent roads in the area, so we're isolated. Industry other than agriculture isn't interested in the land."

"I'm not very good at valuing land or commodities. I'm used to working with businesses in cities where valuing can be done by a trained professional." There was a sigh at the other end of the line.

"Here's the thing," said JJ. "I don't trust anyone around here. And if I contact the big city financial planners, they're going to smell money and take advantage of me."

"OK, why me? I am a big city financial planner." While JJ was talking I turned my chair around and was looking out the window. It was a beautiful sunny day outside. Maybe I needed to get out of the office? I was sort of daydreaming.

"Brett says you're honest and quick."

So far, I'd heard nothing to interest me in driving to this backwoods town. But, it was as if the phone was glued to my hand. The Georgia rural location had brought back a memory of an incident nearly 40 years ago. This call had spooked me to think about it. My mind was drifting again. A jolt brought me back to the present. I decided to continue my questioning.

"You haven't told me your problem. If it's just to avoid paying income tax or estate tax, we can handle that remotely. We can even talk face-to-face over the web unless you don't have that capability. I don't see why I have to come up there."

"Arthur, it's not just that I want to avoid paying taxes. That definitely concerns me, but my real problem is my sons. Both of them want to run the company. Arthur, living in the South, you do understand blood and first born, correct?"

"Yes, go on." My brain said hang up, but my mouth overrode it. The word blood really spooked me. What was going on with me?

"Well, they're twins, born minutes apart. The oldest feels he should run the company but the second-born is more aggressive and works harder. I love my sons. I don't know what to do. I'm worried how my family will take care of the business let alone pay any estate taxes due. It's driving me crazy. I need you to come up here and meet everyone and help me figure this out."

I just had one case to wind up, nothing was stopping me. All the other plans were passed on to the firm's financial planners whom I'd hired and trained. Did I really care about this guy's problems? Why was I continuing to talk to him? Something was pulling me in. I couldn't resist. Why, why?

"JJ, I did a map search while we talked. It's going to take me most of a day to get up there. The only hotel within 50 miles is the Dixieland Motel and Court, built in 1948. I'll have to charge you by the day and I'll have to find a local place to stay."

"I'll be glad to pay you by the day, and you can stay with us. It's a big old family home. It's got six bedrooms and only my wife and I live in the house. How much do you charge per day, Arthur?"

I felt that the fee would be more than he was expecting. What would be his reaction? I heard a low whistle. The rate was high to cover inconvenience and long-distance office support that would be necessary. Would the fee turn him off?

He said finally, "That much?"

I gave him a good Southern answer, "Yep."

There was a pause, and then JJ agreed. Too fast, it hit me in the stomach. There was more to this than he was telling me.

"How many days do you expect this will take?"

Planning came very naturally to me no matter how hard or complicated the case. "Probably a minimum of two days of travel, one up and one back, plus two days to get a feel for the situation and write the plan. On the fourth day, I'll present the plan. If meetings are required with your professional advisors, that will be extra but at a different rate. All of my financial plans are custom designed. My staff will gather data from you before you see me. My staff's time is included in my five-day fee. Their work lets me move more quickly when we meet. A preliminary plan with alternatives is laid out before I arrive. While I am driving I think through all the alternatives. There is no charge until I leave Tampa."

Actually the daily fee is quite reasonable when you take this into consideration, I thought to myself.

"What's next?"

Wow, why did he agree so quickly? The daily fee was on the high side. He must really need me. OK, I thought let's move on.

I explained a few things. He agreed, and the financial planning process began.

First, there was an engagement letter that spelled out what our business arrangement was and what he wanted me to accomplish. I've done quite a few business succession cases. Fortunately, the basic language was already outlined in my computer. Next, upon agreement, he would have to pay 60 percent of the five-day fee. As soon as the fee was received, my staff would start gathering as much data as possible. This was critical. Client cooperation was a requirement. If he wasn't cooperative, 50 percent of the money paid would be refunded and we'd part company. There were no exceptions.

It wasn't long after the engagement letter was sent that JJ's check arrived. Also enclosed were legal authorizations. He agreed to verbally inform both his CPA and attorney to provide me with any needed information. His written authorizations were then sent to those advisors with a cover letter from me.

It took two weeks for my staff to gather all the data and organize it. They're great. They know just what to do. When they finished, I had two sets of data, one for JJ and one for his corporation.

Before I left, I called JJ's CPA, Gale James, and discussed JJ's personal and business tax returns for the past three years. They were part of the data set gathered by my staff. His CPA, who lived in Birmingham, could access JJ's computer. Gale visited JJ yearly to review the returns with him. His accounting remained basically unchanged

8

from year to year with the exception of additional land purchases and growing investment in additional acreage of various crops.

As we talked, Gale told me how wealthy JJ and his corporation had become. She professed to have no idea how the IRS would value the business. When I asked her how important JJ was to the running of the business, she laughed and explained that JJ's daddy ran the business until he died, which wasn't that many years ago. Since then, JJ's two sons have run the daily operations of the business.

"JJ was far more interested in keeping up with the University of Georgia football team. JJ and his wife are all southern charm. Wait until you see the house." Whether I wanted it or not, I got a full description from Gale of JJ's home and his wife's talents for restoring it.

"What about his two sons? How well are they managing the business?" I inquired when she took a breath.

"Arthur, that's where your problem is. JJ, of course, has control of the business. They're both interested in the business, jockeying to be named heir apparent. They both want to run it. JJ set them up to compete with each other. You'll have your hands full. They'll watch you like a hawk."

It became even more apparent that JJ didn't trust any locals either when I learned his attorney, Len Cross, was in Atlanta. The attorney had drafted a basic package of wills and trusts. In addition, at his suggestion, JJ and his wife had agreed to an irrevocable life insurance trust and funded it some years ago with a fair amount of second-to-die (survivorship life) insurance.

Good basic planning, I thought.

My next move was a phone call to Len, JJ's attorney. He chuckled at my suggestion that dealing with JJ was like shooting at a moving target. Like the CPA, Len acknowledged that he had no way to value the corporation.

Then he began talking about JJ. Good, there would be more sophisticated planning on the horizon, and I would need his cooperation.

He went on to explain that JJ likes to have breakfast or lunch with his fraternity brothers from the University of Georgia. "All his

Kappa Alpha fraternity brothers are well-positioned in Georgia politics and live in a dozen small towns within a 20 to 30 mile radius of his home. The good ole boy network tells him who's in financial trouble, who's tired of farming and who wants to sell."

Remain quiet, you never learn anything when you talk. Len continued.

"JJ is a vulture," he explained. "He knows how to buy land based on its usage. Arthur, he seems easy going, but he's like a fox in a hen house. He has access to plenty of cash and buying at a deep discount is his hobby. The land starts making money immediately. Sometimes, he sells off the existing trees to the paper mills, and then somehow, he gets a grant from the State of Georgia to replant the trees." Len supposed that JJ's significant contributions to UGA gave him some advantage over others in the grant process given his clout with certain members of the State's committee.

That's why he had his two sons running the day-to-day operations; he didn't want to. His sons didn't realize that it was JJ who was building the business, not them. This was a different impression of JJ than the one the CPA had given me.

The corporation was a regular corporation, not an 'S' corporation. The corporation owned all of the land, all the equipment, and the processing plants. The corporation, Lancaster, Inc., was formed by JJ's father. JJ became sole owner of all the outstanding shares of the corporation upon his father's death.

With the preliminary work done, I gave JJ a call. "JJ, this is Arthur. I'm ready to see you. When is a good time?"

"Can you come next Monday?" he asked.

"Sure, I can be there about three o'clock in the afternoon. I have a map to your house."

"See you then."

This was the briefest phone call with a client I'd ever had. Something else was going on. Because I felt that this case would take all my concentration, I told Silvia at my office not to contact me unless there was an emergency. What was ahead of me? I know, I know. At first I never considered taking on this client, but it was too late now to back out. Monday was only few days away. On the bright side, I'd see a part of the country that I'd never seen before once I got off of the interstate.

The remainder of the week passed quickly, along with the weekend. Bright and early Monday, downtown Tampa was already in my rear view mirror.

CHAPTER TWO

Most people don't realize how long it takes to drive from Tampa into Georgia. Flying would be preferable, but it didn't make much sense. Even the puddle jumper airlines didn't get close to JJ's town.

It took almost four hours to get to Valdosta, Georgia. Then it was about 60 miles further on the interstate. Then after that it was local roads after leaving the interstate. At first the local road was a four-lane divided highway, but soon it became two lanes and continued through the rolling countryside. JJ had warned me there wasn't much on the road and he was right as it passed through small towns separated by crops and grazing cattle.

As I drove, JJ's data and preliminary planning kept whirling through my brain. It was fermenting. JJ had asked me to keep all the personal data and Lancaster data confidential. My laptop was Internet accessible, but it was encrypted. Someone who was good might be able to hack into it. JJ was reassured that the computer would be in my possession most of the time and mainly off. He was happy when I told him all the hard copy information was at my office and I took limited handwritten notes. He wasn't the first client worried about privacy issues.

The rolling countryside of rural Georgia almost put me to sleep. I should've brought a thermal mug of coffee with me. There wasn't anywhere to stop. The towns got smaller and smaller. The road was two lanes but in pretty good shape. I am sure JJ made sure the State of Georgia knew his trucks had to get his commodities to I-75 or other points.

The trip brought back memories of traveling with my parents from Chicago to Florida as a young boy in the 1950s. There were no interstates, so we slowly rambled through rural Georgia on an assortment of two-lane highways. The car, like most cars at that time, wasn't air conditioned. The smell of the land engulfed the car. Life in Georgia was so different from what I was used to, and it still is, even now. Not good or bad, but different. That was expected, even 60 years later.

Getting closer, JJ's town appeared in the distance as I passed over a small hill. My brain came alive again.

The house was big, old and just south of town per the on-line map and JJ's description. The house looked like it had been built before the Civil War. As I walked toward the wide front porch, the house looked perfectly restored. JJ was on the porch, waiting for me. I smiled. "JJ, have you been waiting long?" It wasn't much of a guess that it was JJ standing there; he looked exactly as expected. He was slightly overweight, about six feet tall with a reddish complexion. He probably played guard or tackle on his high school football team. He was wearing a much worn UGA hat and smiling.

"No, Arthur, I had one of my sharecroppers watching for you about 10 miles down the road. I told him to watch for a car with a Florida tag. Only locals use this road."

Damn, did people use "sharecropper" as a word anymore? I had stepped back in time. There were many Confederate flags along the last part of my drive.

"Arthur, bring your bags in the house. Sarah Jane is expecting you. How was the drive?"

The Parlor

"Uneventful."

He grinned in response and positively laughed.

"The last time anything eventful happened around here was when Sherman rode through," JJ replied.

This time, I laughed and asked, "Did Sherman come through here?"

"No, nor did his army, but everyone wants to blame their plight on the Union General. They stayed well north of here."

It has been over 150 years since the start of a very bloody war. It still echoes through the generations in the South.

At the entryway a magnificent curved stairway lead to the second floor.

"Arthur, put your bags down. Cinnamon will take them up to your room. Sarah Jane is waiting in the parlor."

Holy crap, more words like "Cinnamon" and "parlor" drew me further back in time. I could imagine what the parlor would look like. But what about a woman named "Cinnamon"?

"There's the powder room if you'd like to freshen up first." Upon entering the little room, something about it crept into my brain. It was very small. It was eerie feeling.

As I came out of the powder room JJ looked at me, "Why Sarah Jane didn't enlarge the room is beyond me. She said it would affect the restoration to change it. It does strange things to people, especially big women. He laughed. Most repeat visitors won't go in there. They use the larger restroom down the hall. Let's go in."

In the parlor, an attractive, sweet looking slender woman turned away from the window where she had been standing and smiled warmly at me. Sarah Jane was about 60 and had aged well. When she held out her hand, I wondered if I should shake it or kiss it? Damn. An unsettling feeling set in, a feeling that I was spiraling back through time.

Then Sarah Jane said, "I'm sure JJ didn't tell you, but the only refreshments we can offer you are strong coffee, Coke products, and water. We don't drink or allow alcohol or Pepsi products in the house. You know, of course, no beverage is more cherished in Georgia than our own Coca-Cola."

Ken Zahn

The history of Coca Cola was well known to me; Coke started in Atlanta. Wine or beer was a non-issue for me. Actually, in keeping with what was flowing through my mind, I expected to be offered a mint julep. What was happening? My brain normally thinks financial planning all the time. Sarah Jane asked me about my trip, and JJ told her what I said, and then what he said. We all laughed together. This all felt like a strange way to start.

Sarah Jane already had various Coke soft drinks, ice and snacks sitting on a table in the room. To break this nonsense thought cycle, I asked for a diet Coke. JJ got me a glass with ice and opened a diet Coke. After gathering drinks and some snacks we sat down in furniture of the period of the house. Not too comfortable.

We sat sipping our beverages and eating a snack quietly for a minute or so. Why not start the conversation with the history of the house?

"You must love this house very much. It looks fully restored."

Sarah Jane said the house was built by the Butlers in 1840. About ten years after the wah-ah (the Civil War, of course), the Butler family fell on hard times. Amazingly, both of the Butler sons had returned uninjured from the War. They found the slaves were gone, plantation fields were choked with weeds, and the house and outbuildings were badly in need of repair. Mr. Butler, confined to a wheelchair and mentally fragile, had been unable to cope while his sons were away at war. Then, one son mysteriously died, and the second son couldn't make a go of running the plantation. It then passed through a few disinterested owners until it was finally purchased by JJ's father and mother.

"JJ may own the land and business, but," Sarah Jane explained, "this is my house. It was in sad shape when I got it. JJ's father lost interest in the house after his wife died. It was restored about fifteen years ago based upon exterior and interior pictures taken by a photographer who came by after the War. JJ had to part with some of his precious cash, but he didn't have a choice." After this discussion Sarah Jane decided we should tour the house. Agreeing quickly got me up from a very uncomfortable chair. To value the house and all

The Parlor

its potential antiques, I took out a small notebook. They both looked at me.

"JJ has never valued the house or the furnishings." Sarah Jane glowed with delight.

Sarah Jane talked and talked; my notebook was filling up. JJ was silent.

The heart-of-pine floors were original, now resurfaced. The plaster walls were mostly original, but much of the woodwork was new.

She said, "This house is in the historical records not only because of its age, but because the Confederate Army used it during the war to recruit soldiers. My great-grandfather was recruited in this very parlor. I'm a member of the United Daughters of the Confederacy, and we hold our local meetings in this parlor."

Sarah Jane decided to start the tour upstairs. JJ and I followed her up the magnificent stairway. The conversation about the up-stairs rooms and the house pulled me into the past. She showed me my room, where my bags were. It was a generous size, with its own bathroom. It originally was the bedroom of one of the sons of the first owner, and it also served as her oldest son's bedroom when he was young.

When the house was built, the upstairs was designed for children and guests. The master bedroom was downstairs in the back of the house. Sarah Jane said the slave quarters used to be in back of the house with the outbuildings where the slaves cooked, but they were torn down years ago. A large study for Mr. Butler, the original owner, was downsized and a modern kitchen added. The house had a com-fortable feel. I told Sara Jane that. She excused herself and said she was going to help Cinnamon prepare a traditional Southern dinner. She told JJ that he had two hours to talk to me. She shook her finger. "No business talk at the dinner table."

JJ and I went into the downsized study, which was still a generous size. It had a distinctively masculine feeling. JJ must have had control over its design. It was a corner room and he opened both windows. I knew what he was up to. He offered me a cigar. I said I didn't smoke.

He asked, "Ever?"

Ken Zahn

"No, never,"

"Wow." He lit up and, despite the open windows, the room quickly smelled like a humidor. Geez, another one of those words again. Unlike the parlor, the leather furniture was comfortable.

"OK, what do you have planned?" I tried not to sound too abrupt.

"Arthur, your staff was pretty pointed about the fact that you liked to work with a time schedule." He outlined the following plan.

JJ said that he and Sarah Jane wanted to chat with me after dinner, to get to know each other. Good start, but little did they know it would give me a chance to talk about his sons. Then early tomorrow morning we would tour the Lancaster land holdings and then go to the office in town, where his sons would meet us. I'd be able to meet them individually during the day, and they would come with their families to JJ and Sarah's house that night.

He asked if I had any suggestions. The smoke must have clouded my brain because I told him that his schedule was fine and that I looked forward to getting started. This turned out to be a mistake on my part.

JJ said, "The third day is wide open, but I understand you've already contacted my attorney and CPA. That means you should be ready to show the plan on the third day."

Actually, it should be the fourth day, better wake up.

"No, JJ, it will probably be the fourth day. I may need the third day to write the plan."

But when he said the "third day" that jarred me into action. "JJ, why haven't you given any of the Lancaster stock to your sons?"

This was a direct question. Gale told me that JJ's father had run the business until he died. JJ told me his father had kept him in the dark about Lancaster. He said his father treated him like President Roosevelt treated Vice-President Truman. Truman hadn't found out about the atomic bomb until President Roosevelt died; the same was true of JJ. His father ran everything his way and never gave him any business information or company stock. But his father gave him the job of buying land to expand the business. His father didn't want him around the office. Over time, JJ became quite adept at the wholesale acquisition of rural Georgia acreage which actually saved the company when his father died. When the IRS tried to use inflated land values, JJ had one land purchase after another at a fraction of what the IRS wanted to use. Then JJ convinced the IRS that his father was the key employee and there was no market for the sale of the old mill. JJ's logical arguments persuaded the IRS to accept a greatly reduced and discounted value of Lancaster, Inc. for estate tax purposes.

"Arthur, I sent the IRS back to Yankeeville with their tails between their legs. So you know what my problem is, don't you?"

"Yes, if you gift stock to family members, you'll have to use fair market value, and your sons will get your low basis. How low is it?"

"It's about 25 percent to 30 percent of fair market value depending on how you value the property. In addition, both Sarah Jane and I have already gifted well over a million dollars to each of our sons over the past years. The annual gift exclusion hasn't put a dent in our net worth. The corporation will get a 100 percent step-up in basis to fair market value when I die."

"I see you've been studying the law."

"Yeah, everyone thinks I'm kind of easygoing, but my mind always goes at full speed. Arthur, what do you think is going to happen to taxes?"

"The marginal income tax rate could increase over time from 35 percent to 40 or more percent. I'm hoping the $5 million exemption for estate taxes and a full step-up in basis will remain in effect. Estate tax rates may also be increased from 35 percent to 50 percent over time. Additionally, the State of Georgia is in trouble right now, which could result in an increase in state income, sales, and death taxes."

"I should have died in 2010 when there was no estate tax."

He continued to moan to himself. "All clients want to reduce both income and estate taxes. I am here to help you substantially reduce estate taxes and allow you to receive a full step-up in basis up to their value at date of death. As an added benefit I will also try to reduce your current income taxes."

The soothing tone made him smile.

Ken Zahn

"Brett told me you helped him from getting skinned by his wife's attorney in divorce court." He sat back in his chair, puffed on his cigar, and said he couldn't wait to see the whole plan. There was no time for chit-chat when I do planning.

"So what gifts have you made to your sons?" He seemed surprised by my direct question. This was part of my more personal fact finder. What was about to happen couldn't be done over the phone. My questions were too pointed.

"Well, they needed houses for their families. I was offered several really nice homes with a limited amount of land. The properties didn't fit into Lancaster, Inc., but were perfect for my sons. There isn't much around here and sometimes people just want out. When they can't find a buyer, they come to me. Besides buying the homes, we modernized them. Sarah Jane wasn't going to be satisfied with a half-ass job. Both houses ended up costing me over a million dollars, which is a lot of money for around here. To gift the houses Sarah Jane and I had to both use our $1 million gift tax exclusion and actually paid some gift taxes years ago."

"What else?" The CPA had told me about the gifting because she had filed the gift tax return. There was more.

"What do you mean what else?"

"The cash." All wealthy clients move cash and collectible assets to family members.

"How do you know about the cash?"

"JJ, I'm trained to read all kinds of financial statements. I'd be a great IRS agent. The cash, JJ?"

"We can each legally give the annual gift exclusion to each son, daughter-in-law, and our one grandchild."

"The hidden cash, JJ?" The room was small enough and my voice strong enough that his head jerked back.

There was a big exhale of smoke, an enormous sigh and a long pause. Be patient.

"Well, sometimes I run into little unusable parcels of land. The owner doesn't want to report the sale to the IRS. I give them cash and the deed is transferred to one of my sons. The transfer taxes are so small that my sons are able to pay them. No one in the property assessor's office suspects the buyer to be anyone other than my sons. Maybe some paperwork doesn't get filed, but the county is happy when all back taxes are paid."

"Anything else?" His face had a worried look. He wasn't smoking anymore.

"No. Don't get me wrong, Arthur, those land deals are very small." Yeah, but he bought the land at a huge discount. How many of these small deals took place and whether they could be combined together crossed my mind. The fact finder information continued on.

"OK, back to the Lancaster stock. Why not give them some stock each year?"

"Arthur, I just can't. My daddy's ways are buried in me. It's in my blood."

Although it was cool in the room, JJ got up and moved an old window fan in the window and turned it on to exhaust. It was bringing in cool air from the opposite window. Some sweat beads appeared when he got up. He wiped them away when he turned away from me. Then he sat down. My questioning continued. My time with him alone was running out. Dinner would be soon.

"If I come up with a plan that involves some stock to be transferred to your sons, will you at least consider it?"

"Maybe," said JJ.

"OK, JJ, what about the University of Georgia?"

"What do you mean?" He wasn't smoking anymore.

"What about gifting stock to UGA?"

"You mean gifting Lancaster stock?"

"Yes."

"I don't want them owning the company."

"There may be a way. Would you consider it?" Keep the pressure on.

"You have some tricks up your sleeve, Arthur. My wife and I love the University. We've had season tickets in the south stands with our friends for years. We even rent a nice house up in Athens for the football weekends so all our friends can come over before and after the game. Costs me a bundle, but it's worth it."

Ken Zahn

"JJ, come on now. Lancaster is writing off the Athens house as a business expense."

"My CPA tell you that?" A few more sweat beads formed.

"No, she doesn't know that. Those Athens business marketing expenses are a bunch of hooey." I lied; maybe she did know about it. This wasn't an issue right now.

"Thank God, she would hang me by my thumbs. Damn, how did you find out?"

"As I said, I'd make a good IRS agent. She released to me a lot of documentation. My staff knows where to look. We've had many clients like you."

I was looking out the window. These "small" transactions bothered me. Was JJ truthful and was that all? Clients don't always tell the truth or divulge all the details.

My preliminary planning thoughts were fitting perfectly together. Trying them out on JJ was the final step. He was thinking about the UGA gift. A large gift might get him multiple tickets on the 50 yard line. He had picked up the cigar. The way he chomped the cigar told me I had made an inroad.

CHAPTER THREE

We talked for awhile about the weather and farming. He had relaxed. About the time JJ finished his cigar, Sarah Jane announced dinner was ready. She wagged her finger at JJ. He wasn't supposed to smoke in the house, especially cigars.

As we left, he quietly put the fan away and closed the windows.

As we walked into the dining room, Sarah Jane's comments about no business at dinner shifted my mind; focus on small talk at dinner. I didn't want to seem all business.

The table was beautifully set for us. Damask napkins, fine china and crystal stemware were complemented by silverware engraved with the family initial, "L". In the kitchen, Sarah Jane was picking up the serving dishes to bring to the table. Everything was spotless. Cinnamon had evidently gone home.

The dinner was just OK. I've never acquired a taste for some overcooked southern vegetables, and, sorry to say, dinner was heavy on vegetables. After a light lunch and a small afternoon snack, hunger made me fill my plate. Sarah Jane was pleased. Toward the end of the meal she commented, "Arthur, you seem to be in pretty good shape. I'm trying to get JJ to watch his diet. His only meal I can control is dinner. His weight is up and the doctor is watching his blood pressure. I know that when he leaves early to meet someone for breakfast, his diet suffers – eggs, bacon, fried potatoes, sausage, biscuits with gravy, you name it. Then, for all I know, it's deep fried chicken at lunch."

JJ looked at me with soulful eyes. "Sarah Jane, I suppose we won't even get banana pudding tonight?"

"No, no dessert. And I think Arthur needs to know about your health. I know why you called him; you're scared. The doctor scared you, didn't he?"

JJ nodded. JJ had lied to me. Over the telephone he told me his health was fine.

Health is a major issue as part of my planning. Rather than let this issue go, without unsettling Sarah Jane, I said, "Tomorrow I'll review both your and JJ's personal health history. I need to know that information, but it will have to wait. Tonight we'll stay away from talking about planning." That statement was a fib; there were other planning issues to cover.

My temper was on edge. I had come all this way, and now I would just have to accept what I found out. JJ's poor health had to be factored into my planning. How bad was his health?

"You're right, Arthur. JJ had breakfast and lunch with his buddies today and I got into a bad mood," Sarah Jane replied.

We went into the parlor for coffee. The coffee needed to be strong. Just sitting around making chit chat makes me sleepy; I am not much of a conversationalist. She poured me a steaming cup, but neither of them joined me. They didn't comment on why they didn't have coffee. Since there was more, the first cup went down quickly. Sarah Jane got up and poured me a second one.

Ready or not, they wouldn't consider the next topic financial planning, but I did. "Tell me about your sons." Sarah Jane's semi-grumpy attitude turned bright and her face glowed with pride. They went to college, joined JJ's fraternity, and came home to join in the family business. She said they were both hard workers. She went on and on about this, so I finally asked, "Are they competitive with each other? How do they get along?"

"What do you mean?"

"Well, they're twins. Are they really close or did they fight with each other a lot when they were growing up?"

"Well, yes, but all boys do that, don't they, JJ?"

He just grumbled.

"How about sports, girls, popularity, you know, those sort of things."

JJ spoke up. The boys had gone out for high school football. Robert, the younger of the sons, beat out John for the quarterback position. John played tight end. They were good enough for a small town high school team. They were above average sized, but too slow. The University sent a scout but he left at half-time. There was no response from UGA. Robert was devastated; John knew the truth.

"What about girls? They must have been popular in high school. Did they marry their high school sweethearts or meet their wives while they were away at school?"

They were both silent. Finally Sarah Jane spoke up. "Arthur, you hit a sore spot. Both John and Robert had an on-and-off puppy love for Cindy Daniels starting in grade school. They really didn't date. This sort of continued in high school. Cindy was very pretty and vivacious. She knew how to keep both of them interested. I don't know how she got enough money to follow them to the University, but she did. She wasn't going to risk having either interested in any of the co-eds." She took a deep breath, and then continued. JJ looked concerned. This had turned serious.

"Cindy did well and became head of her sorority. She kept both of them on a string by making sure they knew she was dating the most popular men on campus. Come break time though, she always asked for a ride home with one of them. They'd all hang out with their old high school friends over the holidays and she'd shift her attention from one to the other."

Ken Zahn

"Her behavior just about drove them and us crazy. One year at the town tree lighting service, I saw her walking arm in arm with both of them. The boys were smiling at her but glaring at each other. Frankly, it seemed clear to us that she wanted to marry into this family. Of course, we didn't dare discuss our feelings with the boys. It made me furious the way she toyed with them, but what could we do?"

She continued, "This three-sided relationship came to a head towards the end of college. John and Robert got into a fight over her, and John had to go to the emergency room. The die was cast when Cindy came to the hospital to be with him. When he asked her to marry him right there in the ER, she accepted. We were surprised, but we weren't surprised. JJ and I believe she always wanted John because he would most likely take over the business and inherit the house."

"So what happened with Robert?"

"He was despondent for awhile but he kept his chin up. After a few months, he started dating and eventually met Susan, his wife. She is a wonderful person and mother. Susan is a bit quiet and likes being a homebody but she's a smart girl."

JJ chimed in. "She keeps a lovely home. The grounds are spectacular. I'm very proud of her. She's president of the local garden club. They keep busy 'beautifying' the town and it makes the family look good."

"But, she is not as pretty as Cindy?" Wow, what was happening to me? I never asked clients such intimate questions. They both flinched.

Sarah Jane answered in a quiet voice. "No."

"But he still wants Cindy, doesn't he?" Was it my temper from earlier tonight or something about the relationship that forced this question? It was nasty. The story of the twins' rivalry over her just compelled me to probe deeper.

"You've cut to the nerve." Sarah Jane said. "JJ and I have seen Cindy working behind the scenes. She still flirts with Robert. She thinks nobody notices it, but we do. It makes us worry about both of our sons' marriages."

"Does he respond?" Bam, right at them. There was a sharp "yes" from Sarah Jane. Geez, what was happening to my brain?

The Parlor

"You don't like Cindy, do you?"

"No, she's a conniving bitch." Sarah Jane blurted out. "I'll be damned if that girl is going to wind up wearing my jewelry and living in this house! Not if I have anything to say about it."

Wow, key planning information was flowing but Sarah Jane was getting very upset. JJ had turned beet red and Sarah Jane was on the verge of hyperventilating.

"Please, sweetheart. You'll make yourself ill." JJ moved over on the sofa and put his arm around her. He looked at me like I was the meanest guy in the world for upsetting her. Damn, I hoped she wasn't going to cry.

I'm sorry for upsetting you Sarah Jane." She shook her head and waved me off.

JJ rubbed her back and Sarah Jane took a deep breath to calm herself. The three of us sat there quietly for a few moments. The only sound in the room was the chiming of the grandfather clock in the corner noting the half hour.

Finally, Sarah Jane looked up and gave me a wan smile. "It's alright Arthur. I know you need to understand these things if you're going to help us. We have a serious problem and now you know it. Your questions hurt but I would never have said this under normal circumstances."

She said that tomorrow night John and Cindy and Robert, Susan and their son, Bobby, were coming to dinner. She wanted me to meet their family. My concern at this point was "how would tomorrow night go?" The rest of the night was mainly small talk about the grandkid's exploits; safe territory. It had been a long day and, excusing myself, I said good night. The day's drive and our difficult conversation had exhausted me.

The financial plan will have to compensate for John dying before Cindy. Under Georgia law she has a right to one-half of the marital property, but John could disinherit her in his will. Inheritances in Georgia are considered separate property which is not subject to equitable division upon divorce. I don't think JJ realized that and he was concerned about the Lancaster stock. Georgia law was different

Ken Zahn

from Florida law. In fact, it was different from almost every other state. Part of the overall plan had to be individual plans for the two sons, including buy-sell arrangements between the two of them. This was the second step in the planning. In addition was the bad news that JJ's health was poor and his two sons were jockeying for position in the company *and* Cindy. This was definitely worse than a messy divorce. Tomorrow was going to be a tough day. I needed all the rest I could get.

It was still early but for some strange reason the cups of strong coffee left me sleepy. They, nor I, knew each other well enough to continue small talk.

Never in all my years as a financial planner had a client ever been asked such a series of nasty questions. Something about being in this house made me do it. Worse yet, Sarah Jane was crying in the kitchen when I went up the stairs. A terrible feeling of doom was affecting me.

CHAPTER FOUR

A hot shower felt good. Now exhaustion was really hitting me. After channel surfing for a few minutes, I turned off the television and looked around. I'd never stayed in such an old home before with such a storied history. The antique furniture was mahogany and beautifully carved and finished. Sarah Jane had told me earlier that the bed was original to the house. It was just barely long enough for me. People in the 1800's were clearly much shorter. My feet grazed the footboard. I slid up and bumped my head. The bed might be a valuable antique fit for a museum but actually sleeping in it presented a challenge. Finally, I curled up. The mattress and bedding was comfy but sleep didn't come easily. The evening's conversation, especially the part about Robert sending John to the hospital, was bothersome. A serious rift between the two brothers had occurred.

When sleep arrived, it was a deep slumber. I've had surgery where I was put under and woke up hours later. It felt like that when a jolt awakened me out of a dream about 5 a.m. The dream hadn't gone away, and although I was awake, the vivid detail was still present. I was in the parlor of the house but I wasn't with JJ and Sarah Jane. I was with an old, sick man, who was confined to a wheelchair. Standing in front of the old man were two young men violently arguing. What was the issue? They kept gesturing out the window. They yelled at the old man and each other. The older man was rolling the wheelchair wheels back and forth. He was clearly agitated. The violent dream left me feeling unhinged. Shaken, I couldn't go back to sleep. The aroma of freshly brewed coffee finally drew me out of bed.

When I heard stirring in the house, I dressed and went downstairs. Voices coming from the dining room told me JJ and Sarah Jane were up.

"Good morning!"

JJ looked over his paper and nodded. Sarah Jane was at the sideboard helping herself to fresh fruit while she spoke to Cinnamon. Her name suited her well. She was tall and slender, with warm brown eyes, and skin to match. She was beautiful.

"Good morning, Arthur. Did you sleep well? This is Cinnamon, our housekeeper."

"Cinnamon, it's a pleasure to meet you. Is Cinnamon your real name?"

"Oh, no, Mr. Arthur," she replied. "That's a long story, and I need to get busy with breakfast right now."

"OK. Oh, and my name's Arthur. Just Arthur."

"Alright, Mr. Arthur." She smiled at me warmly and went back into the kitchen.

JJ wanted to leave right away but Sarah Jane cut him off. She told him breakfast was ready. "You'd better stay away from the downtown diner. I know you'd just love to go down there and load up on cheese grits!" JJ couldn't help but laugh. "Can we at least have coffee with whatever you're serving?"

"Of course."

The Parlor

We sat at the dining room table while Cinnamon brought our breakfast. JJ's face lengthened as he looked at his whole grain cereal, blueberries and toast. Sarah Jane was right. He'd rather be at the diner.

The dream still bothered me. We were all on our second cup of coffee when I asked them to tell me more about the house and the Butler family. Sarah Jane said that the Butler wedding had been the biggest social event of the decade. "Lily Butler was the belle of the ball around here. That's her portrait hanging over the fireplace there." I turned around and saw an oil painting of a beautiful young woman with raven hair, deep blue eyes and a shy smile. She seemed to be gazing right at me. "We found that wrapped in linen up in the attic when we moved in," Sarah Jane said. "Unfortunately, about a year after their wedding, she died giving birth to their twin sons. Mr. Butler never remarried. Local lore has it that he was devastated at losing her. Then when his boys were in their late teens, they were off to War for four years. While they were gone, Mr. Butler had a terrible accident that left him in a wheelchair and enfeebled."

JJ broke in, "He was injured trying to save his horses. One of his barns caught fire in the night and he was out there getting the horses out with the help. A beam collapsed and crushed his legs and the horse he was leading panicked, reared up and kicked him in the head. He was lucky to survive."

Thankfully, both sons came home but one died shortly thereafter. I asked Sarah Jane which of the sons had died and why. She said she didn't know. Sensing that she didn't want to tell me, I tried another angle.

"Most old houses have ghosts, Sarah Jane. Any ghost stories about this house?"

"Arthur, you have to be kidding," she responded with a half laugh.

JJ was expressionless. He concentrated on stirring his third cup of coffee.

I let her think I was kidding about the ghosts, but her laugh has a distributing uncertainty about it. Something had happened in the house years ago, that was certain. "Well," JJ said, "Let's get going. We're burning daylight here."

Ken Zahn

After breakfast, JJ and I left in his truck. It was a beauty, a big black Ford 250 loaded with every comfort, leather seats, satellite radio and Bluetooth. Unfortunately, it had a smoky smell. JJ seemed to be doing everything he could to hasten his demise.

We wandered down back roads, some paved and some unpaved, passing one farm after another. "Looks like these farms were once individually owned. Now Lancaster owns them all?" I asked JJ.

"Right." He wasn't saying much that morning. Was he worried about something? Sarah Jane was smiling, no tears this morning.

"Some of these houses look lived in but they don't look like they're in very good shape?"

"Well, when I buy these people out, I buy the whole package including the house. I tell them they can stay in the house until the owner and his spouse die. When they die, I have another side business that completely tears the house apart. Much of the wood is reusable with a high resale price. You know, people hid things behind walls and floors. I can't tell you what we have found."

Actually these people were tenants. Sharecropping is where the landowner allows the tenant to use the land in return for a share of the crop produced on the land. JJ's company used the land right up to the tenant's house. Most didn't even have room for a vegetable garden. Rather than call them tenants, he called them sharecroppers. Leave it at that, there were bigger issues to solve.

Because the sun was still low in the sky, it told me that we were driving in a circle around the town. We would probably end up back at JJ's house before we went into town. I was almost right about this when JJ said, "Arthur, we're almost back to the house, but I'm taking the shortcut into town. Not much to look at here. The land is pretty flat around here."

"I'm impressed by the amount of land you own, and you own it free and clear. I can't figure the acreage, but it's a lot." He kind of laughed. That laugh again. It had a haughty tone.

Driving around was boring for JJ because he already owned all the land we had seen. He was in his element when he wheeled and dealed to buy land as cheaply as possible. That's where the haughty tone came from. This was great fun for him and he loved it.

"What was the town like?"

"The town isn't much. It's the biggest town around but it has slipped. Some of that is my fault. If young people don't work for me, the other available jobs are for minimal wages and no benefits. So they move away, and all the small businesses in town are struggling. No new businesses are moving in. The population is way down."

"What about doctors and medical facilities?" I asked.

"In a minute, you'll see it."

Just south of town there was a doctor's office with a sign that said "Emergency Room." I said, "That's it?" It was a house built around 1960. Not well kept up, and the sign was wooden with faded lettering. I hope I don't have a medical emergency while I am here.

"Yeah, and at night he turns the light off and the sign out front says 'Do not disturb.' He means it. The mayor confronted him, and he told the mayor to mind his own business. The doctor has told everyone that if they bug him, he'll just leave town. There is a little community hospital about 20 miles from here."

"JJ, this isn't the doctor you're seeing, is it? Please tell me no."

"Actually, I see doctors in Athens. One of them was my college fraternity brother."

"OK, so how's your health?"

This was the best time to ask him. We were alone. He was quiet because his poor health was on his mind. He knew he had to respond to me today.

"My heart is bad. I told Sarah Jane it's hypertension and the medicine I take is to control my blood pressure. It's a lie. I need a major heart operation, but I'm afraid I won't come out of it. So, I've put it off, but it can't wait any longer." He stared straight ahead and let out a big sigh. Bam, the truth came out. Bad news for long-term financial planning techniques.

"Why didn't you tell me?"

"I was afraid you wouldn't come. I'm desperate to get these things settled and have you help us. We need a plan in place before I go under the knife. If you come up with one that Sarah Jane and I can accept, we'll do whatever needs doing right away. If we have to go to Atlanta to meet with my attorney and to Birmingham to see the CPA, we'll make it happen."

At this moment I needed to keep my temper under control. "Frankly, JJ, I wish you had told me. It puts more pressure on me. Some big planning firms might take a month or two to come up with a worthwhile plan to even present to you." I just had lunch with one of my financial planning buddies and he said it took his firm months to come up with a sophisticated, comprehensive plan.

"Arthur, if I had told you, would you have come?" It came out pleadingly.

"Probably not. I'm getting old and don't like to work under pressure. This may take longer than I anticipated. We may have to go to Atlanta. That may mean some rescheduling of my next week's activities."

"I understand. You're my last hope."

"OK. From here on, you must be perfectly honest with me."

Damn. I had some idea of how to solve his situation, but I needed time. Last night's dream wouldn't go away and was concerning me about JJ's two sons. Those two boys in my dream arguing in the parlor still bothered me.

"Thank you, Arthur. Please don't say anything to Sarah Jane about my heart yet. I'll tell her when the time is right."

We drove into town. Time seemed to have stood still there since Ike was President. It gave me an eerie feeling to pass shop windows filled with merchandise that seemed outdated. In Tampa, these places would be run by a thrift shop.

The historic and forlorn looking textile mill that JJ had told me about sat near the middle of the faded town.

"What's happening with the old mill, JJ?"

"I can't tear it down. I sold off all the equipment for scrap. We store items we need in our processing business, including inventory, and I occasionally rent out storage space. It's still in pretty good shape, and the city and county have basically taken it off the tax rolls."

The Parlor

"Why?"

"They're still hopeful some business will want to move here. No other buildings can be used for industrial space. If I tear it down, they have no hope. When I threatened to tear it down, they reduced the assessed county tax value to a minimum value. It is significantly less than its fair market value."

Next to the textile mill, JJ had what he called his processing plants. They weren't much; a bunch of small warehouses with minimal equipment to sort and package the field crops. All of the buildings had loading docks. An overhead rollup door in the back of the old mill was opened to a space where excess crops could be stored on pallets until processed. Some workers were bustling around. I told him it looked efficient. He nodded his head.

"Actually Arthur, my father designed most of this. I added a few modifications after the mill closed. I never would have torn it down."

This man had business savvy. I changed the subject.

"So what do your sons do?"

"Well, they're like order-takers for our inventory. We have an established relationship with buyers. A lot of this is done on the computer these days."

"JJ, please tell me what your sons really do?" There was an edge to my voice. Something deep down was bothering me.

Once again, JJ focused on something far away while looking through the dusty windshield of the pickup truck. "Don't tell Sarah Jane, but not much. They talk big, but I have people in place that run the day-to-day operations. The boys are spoiled. They never got much red clay under their fingernails. They come in late, check on their portion of the operations, take long bullshit lunches with their buddies at the local diner, come back to check things out, and go home early."

The truth eased out, and everything that I learned from JJ's attorney about JJ's sons was beginning to make more sense.

"Do they realize why the business is so profitable, JJ?"

"What do you mean?"

JJ's CPA, Gale, had supplied me with profit and loss statements for the prior three years.

Ken Zahn

Everything Lancaster owns was purchased at deep discounts years ago before commodity prices rose and land became more expensive.

"Well, sort of. Arthur, I need you to question them hard. After last night Sarah Jane and I understand your no-nonsense questioning. Sarah Jane trusts you after last night. The issue is more than me dying. She understands why you questioned her so hard. We need your help with our sons."

His sons were a concern. There was friction. JJ was the glue that kept Lancaster together. "Who do I meet first?" As soon as the words came out I knew I had made a terrible mistake yesterday.

"After we tour the office and I introduce you to some key personnel, you'll meet with John," he replied.

"He's the oldest?"

"Yes, by a minute. John and Robert are identical twins. When they were little, Sarah Jane and I had to dress them differently so we could tell them apart. They're mirror images."

"After that, let's have lunch, but not with your sons. Lunch will give me time to think about what John said before I see Robert. Since they're coming to dinner tonight, let's use it as a reason for not lunching together."

"Right, if you say so. Sounds like a plan." He was completely in the dark with this emotional issue.

If we had lunch with John, my mistake would worsen the situation. Both boys should have been met together initially, not separately. The meeting should have been with just them, not JJ. Meeting John first, then Robert second, indicated "first blood" to Robert. Deep down I was mad at myself for not rescheduling the day. Robert wouldn't like to be second. It was too late to undo what was done; everything was all set up. Even if I tried to change it yesterday, Robert would have already known he was scheduled second. That was bad news for the afternoon interview.

CHAPTER FIVE

Lancaster, Inc. was housed in an old two story yellow brick building next to the courthouse. We parked out front. As we entered the reception area, everyone's head turned. After brief introductions, JJ motioned me into his office. It looked as if nothing had changed from when JJ's fa-  ther died. The calendars on the walls came from various cotton mills. JJ had no use for an office. "Okay, I have some work to do. Betty will take you to John's office." JJ called his secretary and asked her to come in. "Betty, this here is Arthur. John's expecting him. Walk him down there and introduce him, then get me some coffee and see if there is a Krispy Kreme left in the break room. You know the kind I like." JJ gave me a shrug and a smirk, "Gotta stoke the furnace. I'm starving." This guy has a death wish for sure. We'd better get this planning done ASAP.

We went down the hall. Old framed black and white photos of the town and Lancaster, Inc. holdings lined the walls. They needed a good dusting. She politely asked how I liked their little town and

I made the appropriate polite answers. John's office door was closed. She knocked.

"Come in," came loudly through the door. She opened the door and we walked into the room.

"John, this is Arthur. Your father said that you're expecting him."

"Sure, thanks. Arthur, have a seat." He stood up and reached across the desk to shake my hand. "Thanks, Betty," he said.

As she closed the door on her way out, I studied John. Tall and slender, he looked very fit, almost like he jogged and worked out at the gym every day. My first impression was that he took much better care of himself than JJ ever had.

JJ's office looked like nothing had been updated since his father had occupied it. John's office was equally dated. He seemed self-conscious about it. "I suppose you have a fancy office down there in Tampa. I can't convince my father to spend a dime upgrading our offices. He doesn't think it's necessary."

This was not the best way to start. JJ was a good businessman and he knew the appearance of the office was immaterial but the function of the office was material. "Well, I guess appearances aren't that important to your dad. He's put in a state-of-the-art computer system that keeps all inventory, sales, cost accounting, and cash-on-hand current. In addition, your CPA can access the system over the net. This sounds pretty state of the art to me. You are functioning at a level beyond your competitors according to your CPA."

"I guess." He didn't sound convinced.

This sounded very shallow if this was all he worried about. The morning was passing and very little had been accomplished.

"John, as you know, I'm a financial planner and I ..."

He interrupted me. "Arthur, I checked you out with my finance professors at the University. They said you had done some pretty impressive planning with big name alumni. But when I checked the web, all I found were articles and speculation about some murders you got involved in. Did you get a lot of business because of that or are you a good planner?"

Nasty retort. Those murder cases continued to haunt me. There were only two, but both made the national press and TV. Financial planners encounter all kinds of clients and cases, but rarely are they called upon to solve a murder.

My first murder case came after I made a reluctant promise to advise an eccentric Florida orange grove owner. The day after I arrived, she was dead. The local investigating sheriff had had a romantic relationship with her. Because of that relationship and the financial mess, the sheriff asked me to help. By the time I solved the murder, two more people were dead. That gets press attention big time. Write-ups in police journals followed. I was dubbed "agent 706". The 706 comes from an IRS Form 706, which is the federal estate tax return required to be filed after the death of wealthy individuals.

A second case was almost a year later. It was a result of the first case. In this case, a lifelong friend of a gulf coast police chief had been murdered. The police chief told me the man had five or six family members with a financial interest in their father's death. He was under tremendous political pressure to solve a case with no solution.

Fortunately, that was the only death in that case. It just heightened my exposure to the national press. That was when the web site was launched to keep track of me. I guess I had become a colorful character. At least the murders had brought attention to the need for comprehensive financial planning.

John's accusation had put me at a disadvantage. In addition, my temper was flaring again. Something had taken root in my mind. He continued on about the murders and my temper cooled. He was wearing himself out and accomplishing nothing.

Finally, he shut up. "Let me just say this. I've been a planner for thirty plus years. Those two cases happened in the last three years. Let's hope it's not the start of a trend!" John laughed at that, but my statement worried me. After a deep breath, my questioning continued. "Let me ask you some planning questions. What would you do if your father died or turned over the business to you?"

Ken Zahn

He'd probably been thinking about it even more than usual once JJ told him that I was coming. He rocked back in his old leather chair and started tapping his fingers together.

"Personally, I would run it more efficiently. I would sell off some of the unproductive land, get the sharecroppers out of those houses on our land, and build a nice corporate office."

"How about buying more land?"

"No way, we have too much already."

Nice office space didn't produce profits. Lancaster clients did business over the phone or via computer. They could work out of the old textile mill if they had to. The land produced their profits.

"You know the old story 'God only made so much land'?"

"You sound just like my father." His chair squeaked as he leaned forward and rested his elbows on his desk. John looked me straight in the eye and had a sullen look on his face.

"Tell me about the kind of courses you took at the University." Finding some substance in him became an issue for me.

He sat up straight and replied, "I majored in business."

"Were any of the business courses agriculture related?" I asked.

"No need. We have those people working for us."

"So you could quarterback this operation better if you were in charge?"

"You know, Arthur, quarterback is exactly the word I used with my wife when I heard you were coming. I've been running my portion of the business more efficiently than my brother has been running his."

"How do you know this?"

"Well, my profits are more than his are."

"What do you handle?"

"Mainly cotton."

"And him?"

"Mainly peanuts, but he's adding corn."

Peanuts took a real hit when a plant in Georgia was found full of salmonella problems a few years ago and cotton was a hot money making item.

"So he might do better going forward."

The Parlor

"No way. I'll never let that happen. If he does, I'll switch some of my acreage to corn." John gave me a menacing grin. Sibling rivalry had reared its ugly head. It was no surprise.

This was getting us nowhere. JJ had told me that John and Robert had no significant responsibilities. JJ or his father had trained the personnel who ran the day to day operations. Those people reported to JJ now. If John didn't show up, no one really cared. So far, all I had heard were negative retorts from John. All he wanted to do was show his brother up. This was a dead end street.

"John, tell me about your family."

That perked him up. "My wife Cindy is the light of my life. We met in grade school and I always knew she was the girl I'd marry." Finally, he said that although Robert had tried to win her heart, he had won out. I had picked up the wedding picture of the two of them that he had on a corner of his desk. John's voice was warm, and he was genuinely smiling. "Not only is she beautiful, she's also clever. And, she has great taste. You should see what she's done with our home. It's fantastic." He went on and on and I thought he'd never finish. He never said a word about winding up in the hospital after the fight with Robert.

"John, any plans to start a family?"

"Cindy and I have decided to wait a few more years. Cindy has her mind made up."

"Have you ever thought of moving to a big city like Atlanta? This is a pretty small town."

"No way. As soon as dad says so, I'm ready to run this organization."

I tried various open-ended financial planning and business questions. The answers were simple one-liners. He clearly thought of himself as the heir apparent and his impatience and smugness wore me down.

"Thanks for your time. See you at dinner." Enough! Arrogance coupled with ignorance really grates on me. He defeated my purpose. I had learned nothing except he couldn't run this company. It was time for lunch and some fresh air. As he opened the door for me, he said "Cindy can't wait to meet you."

Ken Zahn

I nodded. He will brag to her how he influenced me. It will be interesting how she tries to play it. John was a nice guy but in over his head and doesn't know it. This interview with John made me want to go home. A sense of hopelessness came over me as I walked down the hall back to JJ's office. Photographs were hanging on the wall. One large one was JJ's father. As I looked at it, was JJ's father spinning in his grave? "Let me out," he was saying.

On our way to lunch, JJ tried to drag out of me what I thought about John. "Seems like a nice guy." When we pulled into the restaurant's parking lot he finally said, "You don't say much, Arthur, do you?"

"No."

The interview crushed my interest in eating. My stomach was churning in the wake of my interview with John. Normally, client interviews excite me. To me, they're fun. Not today. A simple salad sounded good. The waitress glared at me. Geez, what now? JJ laughed.

"No one orders just a simple salad around here."

JJ ordered something Sarah Jane wouldn't approve of. I silently ate my salad while he munched on deep fried chicken, baked beans and coleslaw. He downed a few buttered rolls. Grease was all over his plate, hands and mouth. The waitress refilled his glass with sweet tea and mine with diet Coke. Various people came by and introduced themselves.

Finally when we were alone and no one was around, I asked, "JJ, what do you think about John running the company when you die?

He almost choked on the chicken. He took a deep drink of sweet tea. "Did John say that?"

"What if he did? Tell me the truth. This is going nowhere fast."

"You can't tell Sarah Jane. You're the only one I can trust."

"Fire away."

"Arthur, he's the nicest boy. He means no harm but can't seem to grow up. Cindy runs his life the way she handled him before their marriage. He doesn't even know it. Oh, he does his job – simple as it is – but he has no vision of the future."

"Does he know how you feel?"

The Parlor

"No, and I don't know how to tell him."

"Now I'll tell you the truth. He can't run the company," I said decisively.

"So what do you propose?"

"Don't know yet, maybe after I talk to Robert something may make sense." JJ eyes were saddened.

"You do know the most famous Pogo cartoon, don't you?" I asked.

"Which one is that?"

Set in the Okefenokee Swamp in southeastern Georgia, the strip was written by cartoonist Walt Kelly. It often engaged in social and political satire through the adventures of its anthropomorphic and funny animal characters. Pogo, the possum, was the wisest resident of the swamp.

I quoted Pogo, "We have met the enemy and he is us. That lives with me every day." JJ lost his appetite and couldn't finish his chicken. I didn't have much to eat myself. Neither of us had much to say after that. We busied ourselves by pushing what remained of our food around on our plates.

After our glasses were drained, JJ called the waitress over and paid the tab. He struggled out of the booth and left a tip on the table. "Meet you out at the truck in a few minutes, Arthur. There are a couple of fellas over there I need to talk to for a second." I went to the restroom and then went outside. The morning had ended badly for both of us.

The SUV was unlocked and I climbed in. We were out in the country. Nobody ever felt the need to lock anything around here.

JJ was excellent at buying property and had a well run, respectable company. Obviously, JJ was doing a terrible job of grooming his sons to succeed him. He certainly wasn't managing their role in the future of his company or his family. He had given his son, John, a job he could do. Due to that, John thought he was capable of running the company. That wasn't true. It was the people JJ and his father had trained plus JJ himself that made the company run well. JJ realized his mistake with his son, but didn't have a solution. There had to be a solution that would get these boys up to speed regarding company operations. In addition, both John and Robert had to feel that they'd gotten the best deal. At the same time, JJ and Sarah Jane's financial future had to be tied to Lancaster, Inc. If all that could be put into one plan, then maybe JJ's father would stop spinning like a top and rest in peace.

CHAPTER SIX

On the way back to the office after lunch, both JJ and I were quiet. We felt the same. There wasn't much to say.

Robert's interview was right after lunch. JJ wasted no time taking me to Robert's office. It was very much like John's. The carpet was faded and worn, the desk beat up, and a few UGA souvenirs on a sagging shelf in the bookcase. And, as JJ had told me, Robert looked almost exactly like John. Robert was sitting behind his desk in an ancient leather chair with cracked armrests. He didn't look very happy. "Son, here's Arthur. See you tonight at the house." With that terse introduction, JJ was gone.

I was still feeling out-of-sorts. When he didn't even shake my hand, I knew this was going to be bad. I just sat down. Not wasting any time, he said, "I see I'm playing second fiddle again."

"What do you mean?" Keeping my cool, the response was to see how badly the interview would go. My client fact finding didn't normally go this way.

"You saw John-boy first. Why don't you and Dad just get it over with?"

It must be tough to be a twin, competing with a mirror image of yourself. How could I get Robert off this second-born track?

"Whatever is on your mind is a figment of your imagination."

"That's bullshit. Mom and Dad want my brother to rule the roost."

"Robert, why don't we start over? Nothing has been settled. That's why your father brought me here. He hired me to be an independent party."

"I don't believe you," Robert said.

"I understand why you could feel that way, but it's the truth." There was a little harshness to my voice. I was still on edge.

Robert was determined to be uncooperative. Why not go to the heart of the matter?

"OK, tell me what your plans are if the company is turned over to you." I kept a positive tone.

"Why should I waste my time answering you?" Geez, what a jerk.

I stood up to calm myself, walked to look out the window and sat down. "Humor me." I glared at him. Before lunch was bad, this was worse. The imagination factor for the proposed financial plan was magnifying exponentially. There was a long pause. Robert glared back at me and I raised my eyebrows quizzically. The pause continued. "Come on, this is your chance. I understand you were once a quarterback. Don't blow it, throw me the ball!" My hands were up like a receiver.

With that, Robert laughed and started to loosen up a bit. "Okay, here's my view of the playing field. When we both came back after college, Dad gave my brother the best land to grow cotton. I got the worst land to grow peanuts. Peanuts are never as profitable as cotton. What made them worse was the bad news with the peanut processing plant problems not far from here a couple of years ago. Dad is letting me try corn. No one here knows how to grow corn. The people around here are stuck in the mud. I did my own research and figured I'd give it a shot."

"What was your field of study at the University?" Back to education again.

"Physical Education."

"PE?" A surprised look crossed my face. There was nothing wrong with PE, but if you were going to run a fair sized company, why not take courses that would prepare you?

"Yeah, I tried out for various sports, but I was never quite good enough. I thought maybe by majoring in PE and being around the good players, I would improve. I was a star in high school."

"Did you take any electives like business management or maybe an AG course?"

"You're kidding. I wasn't going to waste my time with those nerdy book learners or manure haulers. I wanted to be around the movers and shakers."

"You mean the jocks."

"Yeah."

Fire the two of them and hire someone to run the company pulsated through my brain. John had at least majored in business management but couldn't manage the Lancaster operations. It seemed that Robert had wasted his University education pursuing a pipe dream. His dream was that he could be a professional athlete. JJ had done some serious harm here. Now he also had destroyed his health and was in danger of leaving his wife and sons with the family and business in chaos. No wonder he called me. Was it too late?

"OK, back to my original question. How would you run this company if you had total control?" Attack the major planning issue, get an answer. One of them had to be capable of running the company. JJ might have to bring in an outsider. That would destroy this family.

He stood up and glared down at me. He was at least six feet tall. He started pacing behind the back of his chair while he talked. I just sat there looking up.

"I'd try to use the computer system more effectively. With two divisions, we fight against each other. Some employees should have been canned when we bought the new computer system. Dad can't do that. Some employees are limited by their education, but may be able to handle another job."

"Do you understand what the computer system can do?"

"Yeah, I get all the reports I need. However, I think I need to spend more time finding out what else we can do with it to improve our operations. Dad never finds time to hear me out about it, though. He's hardly in the office." With that said, Robert got up and walked over to the credenza. "Care for a cup of coffee?"

Strange move. Coffee was the last thing I needed but it seemed to be a conciliatory gesture. "Black, no sugar. Thanks." After handing me a cup, Robert sat in his desk chair and swiveled it to look out the window. "My granddad created all this. Quite a legacy."

He appeared to be pleased with his solution. Now it was my time to attack. Was he ready?

"What about John?" That was the next issue. The two would never work together in this environment. Robert turned to face me. This put him on the edge. He was gripping the armrest and scowling at me. Would he explode? Would he tell the truth?

"What do you mean? With two divisions, Dad's got us set up to fight against each other. Seems that's the way he likes it." He was trying to buy time. I went right back at him.

"What would you have him do if you were in total charge?" Bam, right between the eyes.

"I'd send him and his damn wife on a cruise around the world," Robert replied angrily. The truth came out. Like last night, an even more personal question came next. How he would react?

"I understand you and Cindy had a fling or two." This was definitely not a normal financial planning interview question. I had ever asked a client this type of question.

It caught him off guard. Surprisingly, his tone softened. "Yeah, but she just used me to get to John." That was a pretty low-keyed response. He shook his head and shrugged.

Go the whole way, ask it invaded my brain. "I understand she's still after you." Where were these thoughts coming from? This was so unlike me.

"What makes you think this is any of your business?" He was livid. He pushed his chair back and stood straight up. "Get out of here before I throw you out. And you can tell my mother that she has nothing to worry about. Cindy fooled me once, I'm not about to let her do it again. God! My parents really think I'm an idiot! Just get out!"

He was about to come around the desk at me. I stood up as if to leave and opened the door to his office. Ordinarily, I would never question a new client like this, but my temper got the best of me. But there was some substance in his parents' concerns. Now his temper got the best of him.

"Robert, you want everyone to hear? If you sit down, I'll close the door," I said loudly to be sure everyone within earshot heard me.

Robert backed up and lowered himself into his chair. He rocked it back and forth so hard that it creaked like an out of tune violin. I closed the door and returned to sit across from him. Both of us glared at each other for a moment. His jaw hardened and he looked like he was going to spit at me.

"Let's get this all out. No holds barred. When you and John were in college, why did you beat him up?"

"What? What has that got to do with anything? What the hell kind of 'planner' are you?" he asked.

"It has to do with you blowing up about me mentioning Cindy. The future is you and your brother. Is the issue your brother or your brother's wife, that's what's bothering me."

"You sure about that?"

"Absolutely. That's why I'm here. Your parents want to do the best for you and John and for the company. Your dad called me to help figure this all out. This is a tough deal, talking about this stuff, but I need to understand if I'm going to help you."

Robert let out an exasperated sigh and shook his head.

"OK, this seems ridiculous to go over all this with you but let me try to explain. I decided that Cindy was just playing me, so I was dating around. Being around the jocks meant there were always plenty of good looking girls to choose from at the University. Cindy could see that I wasn't interested in her. She made one more big play for me in front of John. She wanted John to think he had a rival. Later, John told me to leave her alone, that I wasn't good enough for her,

Ken Zahn

that all I could attract was what the jocks had no use for anymore. I blew up. I beat the crap out of him."

"So how did you feel afterwards?" This was critical.

"I was glad I did it, but Mom and Dad nearly took me out of school." So he really wasn't sorry.

"How do you get along now?" What would dinner be like?

"Barely. We never do anything together besides events like tonight."

"Have you discussed this with your dad?"

"Did Dad tell you?"

"No, what?"

"Well, when I found out you were coming, I met with Dad and John at the house. I lost it again. I yelled and screamed that I deserved to run the operation. That John didn't have the brains and he sure didn't have the guts to run this company the way it needs to be run. You know, he lost out to me to be the quarterback of the high school team. Frankly, he was better than I was, but he just wouldn't stand up for himself. Now Cindy's the one pushing him around. It's laughable to think he could run the company."

"So, what happened at the house?"

"Nothing. They both just looked at me. That made me more furious. I yelled and screamed some more. That's why I feel you're just wasting my time. Dad is going to let John run the company."

My hair stood on end. Flashes from my dream from last night were giving me a sickening feeling. The men in the dream were dressed the way men dressed in the mid-1860s. I could see one of them yelling and screaming and gesturing out the window in the parlor.

"Robert, were you all in the parlor when this happened?" The house knew what was going to happen. It had heard it before.

"Yeah, why?" Robert looked puzzled.

"Just how mad did you get?" Was he mad enough to kill?

"What do you mean?"

"Mad enough to beat John up again?"

Robert paused for a moment before he answered. Then he sighed deeply and responded, "I guess so. John just sat there. Damn him. What difference does a minute make?"

The Parlor

"You mean he is the first born."

"Yes."

He looked exhausted. I was feeling very uneasy; the flashes of the dream continued. I needed to know what happened in that house almost 150 years ago. All of a sudden, I was completely calm. He had told me how to complete the financial plan. This was a bad way to end the interview, on such a sour note, so I asked about his family.

He didn't say much about his wife, but he told me about his six-year-old son, Bobby. He said that almost every afternoon he went home to play football with his son. He had great plans to make his Bobby good enough to play at the University level. As Robert went on and on, I drifted back into the dream. I have a multi-track mind. I can listen, understand, and remember what the other person said while thinking about two or three other situations. Right now, however, only one other situation ran through my mind. Finally he thanked me for listening to him. He had also calmed down.

Deep down, Cindy was still a concern. He may be lying. He said almost nothing about his wife. The only photos on his desk were of his son playing football. I take note of everything.

JJ saw me coming out of Robert's door and waved me into his office. He closed the door.

"Arthur, what happened in there? We all heard Robert yelling at you. He always had a temper."

"We were talking about Cindy and the meeting with the boys at the house before my arrival. You didn't tell me about the confrontation in the parlor."

JJ should have told me about the confrontation. If I had met only with JJ and Sarah Jane I would never have known about the real planning issues. The two sons, not the IRS, were the problem.

"Geez, you really got into it."

"This is why you made me come here, isn't it? You don't have an estate tax problem; you have a family problem."

"What do you want to do?" He could see I was upset. I am a good planner, but I am not good with people's emotions. But why was I asking all these emotional questions?

Ken Zahn

"I want to go back to the house."

On the way, we were quiet again. JJ asked me not to say anything to Sarah Jane about Robert. She had a big dinner planned. I told JJ that Robert had calmed down and would behave tonight. He asked why.

"He blew off all his steam. He won't embarrass himself in front of his mother."

"Arthur, are you going to calm down?"

I told JJ that I wanted to be alone for the remainder of the afternoon and was going to go back into town to wander around and think about his situation. It was a lie, but he bought it. My temper was still alive. I hadn't calmed down. You can't think straight when your temper is flaring.

I needed someone who could tell me what had happened in the house years ago. I had a feeling that there was another reason I was here. Something had drawn me here.

CHAPTER SEVEN

A sense of dread came over me as the town came into view. Who would be the best source of local history going back that many years? The Sheriff would know who that person was. Thinking about the Sheriff brought back bad vibes of the first murder case I'd been involved in. At least no one was dead yet.

His office had to be on Main Street. A small modern building had "Sheriff's Office" on it. An American flag hung out front of the building. I parked in front and walked in. An attractive young woman was working at a metal desk behind a long Formica counter. Apparently she was a combination receptionist and dispatcher. No one else was around.

She barely looked up from her stack of paperwork. "Yes?"

"I want to see the Sheriff."

"Why?"

"It has to do with Lancaster." Her head bounced up. Now she was paying attention. She gave me the once over.

"You must be Arthur. Go on back. All he's doing is resting his eyes."

"Are you going to announce me?"

"No, I'm too busy. If he doesn't want to talk to you, he'll throw you out." She continued to work on her stack of paperwork. This was no southern belle. She was tough enough to work in New York. If this was what the receptionist was like, how would the Sheriff react to me?

As I approached his office, I heard snoring. I knocked softly on the half-opened door, then pushed it completely open and entered. He was asleep with his mouth open and his feet propped up on his desk. With every snore, his crossed arms rose and fell against his ample belly. He didn't hear me.

"Sheriff." He opened his eyes and swung his feet to the floor.

"Who in ding blazes are you? How'd you get in here? That dingbat worthless girl let you through?"

"Sheriff, my name is Arthur. I'm in town to work with Mr. Lancaster."

"Oh, that's different. I heard you were coming. It's all around town."

"How did that happen?"

"It's a small town." I was getting use to attention being paid to my activities. Somehow the bloggers were following me. Still, that's the same phrase I heard when I got involved in the other murder cases. The Sheriff went on.

"You're almost as famous as Sherman was when he came through here."

"Thank you, Sheriff." I needed a lead and he had given me one. "May I sit down?" He nodded and waived me to a chair. He was wondering why I had come calling.

"Listen, Sheriff, I'm glad you brought that no-good Union General up. I am sort of a Civil War history buff. I understand from Mr. and Mrs. Lancaster that a lot of local Civil War history took place in their house."

"Yep, it's the most famous house around here."

Then he corrected me. "Arthur, don't refer to the War as the Civil War. Refer to it as the War Between the States. You sound too much like a Yankee."

"You're right. Thanks. Is there anyone in town who knows the history of the house? The Lancasters are vague about its history."

"Yes, Miss Edith Faircloth."

"Is it possible to see her?"

"I doubt it."

"Why?"

"She doesn't see anyone anymore. She's nearly blind and has had some bad episodes of skin cancer. She says she wants to die in peace. No one knows how old she is because there was a fire and all the city birth records were destroyed. She knows her age but it's her secret."

"I'd still like to see her. Can you contact her?"

"OK, but I don't think it will do any good. She won't see anyone from town; I don't know why she'd see a stranger."

"Tell her my name and that I'm staying at the Butler house. As you say, it is a small town and she'll know who I am."

"The Butler house? I see you know something about the place."

"Yep." Why say more?

He glared at me, because he didn't want to make the call, but then reluctantly he made the call. Predictably, Miss Edith had a housekeeper. In a loud voice, the Sheriff repeatedly told the housekeeper what I wanted. The housekeeper protested loudly, "No, no." Then there was silence at the other end of the line. Looking around at the government issue surroundings made me glad I'd never become a civil servant. It was too dreary and institutional for me with the cold fluorescent lighting and uniformly ugly furnishings. The Sheriff was focused on his computer screen, tapping away on his keyboard while we waited. He was probably checking his e-mail. Finally, he grunted into the phone and hung up. Evidently, Miss Edith had agreed.

"Harriet says that Miss Edith will see you only if you come now."

"OK, Sheriff, where's her house?"

"Not so fast. I know who you are. You've solved a couple of murders. You are all over the Internet. I even called the Sheriff in Florida. He was quite talkative about the murder case he involved you in. He really likes and respects you."

"Sheriff, I need to leave now."

"You want to question Miss Edith about the Butler murder?"

"What murder?"

Ken Zahn

"You don't know, do you? One of the Butler boys was found dead in his bedroom. No one was ever accused of the crime. It was swept under the rug by the Sheriff at that time. Many of the boys who came back after the War were not all right mentally. No one wanted the murder to be investigated, especially Mr. Butler. Mr. Butler never expected one of his sons to return, much less both of them."

"This is the first I've heard about a murder."

"Yeah, I suspected the Lancasters wouldn't say anything about it. Here's the deal. I would like to know what you find out. This is the most interesting thing that has happened around here in years."

"Here's my deal," I replied. "You keep your mouth closed about me seeing Miss Edith, about the house, and the Butler murder. Then you will be kept informed. If this gets out, I won't tell you anything. In addition, I may need your help. Now tell me how to get to her house."

He nodded his head, gave me directions, and walked me to the door. He glared at the receptionist as I left.

Miss Edith's house wasn't far. It was a plain, one story 1930s era house with a well-kept yard. On the left side, there was a narrow driveway leading to a detached garage with big double wooden doors. I pulled into the driveway and parked. As I walked toward the front door, the door flew open and the housekeeper glared at me.

"My name is Arthur and..."

She cut me off.

"I know who you are. Miss Edith will see you. Don't tire her out. It's almost time for her nap."

Harriet led me into a sitting room off the entry hall. The windows were framed by faded red brocade draperies, open as far as possible to let in the light. Miss Edith sat in a tattered silk armchair between the windows. Harriet pointed to a delicate antique wood chair across from her. I sat down gingerly. She gave me a final grimace and left the room.

Miss Edith looked exactly as expected. She was very tiny and old; I'd guess at least 100. Her hair was arranged to cover part of her face, which was badly disfigured by the skin cancer.

The Parlor

In a surprisingly strong voice she said, "So you are the infamous Arthur." Evidently someone told her about the murder cases. I found out later it was Cinnamon.

"Miss Edith, I'm infamous for the wrong reasons. I'd rather solve people's problems than watch them die." My response was based on the assumption that she was referring to the murder cases.

"So you want to talk about the Butler house, do you? I haven't heard it referred to by the original name in years. Because of its history people stopped referring to it by name after JJ bought the house and Sarah Jane restored it."

"The Sheriff told me you knew everything about its history."

"Why do you want to know?" She seemed to look right through me and I shifted nervously in the tiny wooden chair. It made a creak that I hoped wasn't a warning that it was about to collapse under my weight. Like the bed that I'd slept in the night before, this antique had been designed for a much smaller person.

With a deep breath, I tried my War Between the States history buff story for the second time and she laughed. Damn, another laugh. Geez, I am usually very good at lying.

Miss Edith firmly tapped her index finger on her armrest. "Arthur, the truth is you want to know about the murder."

"Well, Miss Edith, I only heard about it thirty minutes ago from the Sheriff. But now that it has come up, yes."

"You came into town today looking for something; you just didn't know what it was, did you?"

"No." I wondered if she could read my mind? Did she know the house had attracted me and was pulling me in?

"You had a dream while you slept last night, didn't you?"

"Yes." Was she psychic?

"What was it about?"

"Well, it was like seeing something that happened in the house at about the time of the Civil War. I woke up with the dream in my head and it won't go away." I had slipped again, but she didn't flinch when I said Civil War. She was too interested in what I had to say.

Ken Zahn

"What did you see?" I could tell from her expression that I'd piqued her curiosity. She leaned forward to hear me better.

"I saw two young men in the parlor of the house. One of the young men was yelling at a man in a wheelchair and gesturing out the window."

"What room are you sleeping in?"

"Why?"

She looked at me.

"The one almost at the top of the stairs."

"The death room." Miss Edith was very solemn.

The hair on my arms stood up. My breath left me. I couldn't speak.

"Arthur, is the bed a four-poster bed with a huge headboard?"

"Yes, Mrs. Lancaster said it was original to the house."

"The death bed." She continued shaking her head.

My heart was pounding. I managed a squeak. "Aaaah." My body had a chill go through it.

"You think the house is telling you something, don't you?"

My voice was a whisper. "Yes." The chair beneath me squeaked loudly when I shifted forward and sent another chill up my spin. I concentrated on my breathing in an effort to calm down.

"Arthur, I am going to tell you what no one else knows." I was intent on learning what had compelled me to seek her out.

This was her story. Mr. and Mrs. Butler had come here in the late 1840s from Charleston, South Carolina. He had sold his rice plantation for a lot of money, and came here to grow cotton. He had ties to both Charleston and Savannah cotton brokers. He bought large tracks of land and the slaves he needed. His wife wanted a grand house and he built her one. Everything worked until Mrs. Butler died giving birth to twin sons. The second son's birth caused her to bleed to death. Mr. Butler was never the same after that, but the plantation thrived. Cotton was king before the War.

Miss Edith took a sip of water and sat quietly for the moment. Then she went on.

Just about the time the boys were reaching manhood, the War broke out. Like Sarah Jane, Miss Edith told me about how the Confederate recruiters had used the parlor to enlist local boys.

Mr. Butler was left alone after both his boys joined the Confederate Army. During the War, he wasn't able to sell cotton overseas. At the War's end, most of his money was gone and his health was failing. He kept his house slaves and sold off the others. With no one to work the fields, weeds and small trees began to take back the land. The fire and subsequent accident diminished him mentally and physically. Then his slaves left him, but to his surprise, both boys came home. Of the two, the older boy had seen the worst of the fighting and was shaken by it. The younger one had become more hardened.

The younger son was aggressive and wanted to find a way to farm the land again, but Mr. Butler wanted the land management to go to the older son. He didn't give the younger son a chance. That was the "rule of blood."

She said, "I believe Mr. Butler still blamed the younger boy for the death of his wife."

I was calmer now. My chair stopped squeaking.

"So what happened?"

"One night, there was an argument in the parlor. The younger boy became violently angry with his father and brother. Within a few days of the argument, the older boy supposedly shot himself in the head at night in the bedroom where you are sleeping. Only Mr. Butler and the younger son were in the house. It was early morning before the Sheriff was informed. There's no way to know what really happened and it's been a mystery ever since. Of course, there was plenty of speculation." Miss Edith sat back in her chair and seemed lost in thought.

"How do you know all of this?" She had me completely enthralled.

"My grandmother was engaged to the older son. He told my grandmother about the argument the night before he died. She told me that there was no way he would have killed himself. They had made plans that night to go to Charleston in a few days and let the younger brother have the land."

"Why would the older brother give up his birthright? Love of the land is inbred in Southerners."

Ken Zahn

"The older brother had seen too much fighting during the War and knew he didn't have the energy to fight his brother and restore the plantation and land."

That was believable. As an officer, he would have seen many men die.

"Did the younger brother know that?"

"She said she didn't think so. The parlor fight was the last straw. The older brother had just made up his mind."

"So, what happened to the younger brother?"

"Nothing. The Sheriff couldn't prove anything. There were no witnesses. Mr. Butler was in failing health and exhausted. He didn't want to pursue the matter. I don't think Mr. Butler wanted to know what had really taken place."

I could tell by the expression on her face that telling me this story was making her reach back to a dark period in her grandmother's life. No one else knew this. It was a very private matter.

"What happened to the younger brother?"

"Mr. Butler had no choice but to give him free rein. The boy tried hard to save the plantation. He borrowed money against the land with his father's consent. Low cotton prices and bad weather worked against him and he kept losing money. Eventually, the banks took the land and house. Fortunately for Mr. Butler, he passed away before that happened. The son had lost everything. The son died a young man in an old body."

"And your grandmother, what happened to her?"

"The younger son had a crush on her, but she never had liked him. She met a man from another town that she married. She moved away and never came back to this town again. She never saw the younger son again either."

I didn't say anything. Quite a story.

"Why do you live here, considering what you know?"

All she said was that it was a long story. After a moment she said, "Arthur, I can feel your concern. What's bothering you?"

"Miss Edith, as soon as I arrived, I felt like tragic things had happened there and were likely to happen again. I can't explain it but I think you just did!"

The Parlor

"Some people are able to sense these things, Arthur."

"Well, if history repeats itself, there's going to be another murder in the house." Leaning forward and whispering, I said, "Robert Lancaster will kill John Lancaster soon."

She gasped. "You don't mean that!"

"I'm here to stop it." My voice had determination in it.

She looked doubtful. Honestly, I was doubtful myself. This really didn't happen in real life, only in books and movies. But Miss Edith's story made sense to me and I knew now why I had the ominous feelings and the bad dream.

"How? What can you do?"

"Well, I can't prove anything, nothing has really happened yet. You're the only person who would believe me. I'll deal with this the only way I can. I have to devise a financial plan that will satisfy both sons."

"Can you do that?"

"At this point, no. The interview with John and Robert Lancaster went badly. Robert lost his temper with me. We came close to blows."

Another gasp. Miss Edith sank back in her chair and seemed worn out.

"Miss Edith, I didn't mean for this to burden you. I'm sorry I came." I stood up to leave.

"Sit yourself down and you listen up. My grandmother would roll over in her grave if I didn't help you. I'm the only one you can talk to."

I glanced at the open doorway. Was Harriet listening?

"Did your housekeeper hear us?"

"No, I'm nearly blind and Harriet can't hear very well. That's why she shouts at everybody. She gets annoyed with nearly everyone who visits. It upsets her routine. She can be a trial but we depend on each other. It's been so long since she's worked for me, I think of her like family."

"If I need to see you, I can't go through the Sheriff. What is your phone number?" She told me her phone number. I wrote it down in my trusty notebook.

Ken Zahn

"Do you ever answer the phone?"

"No. I don't. I'm not so quick on my feet anymore. I'll tell Harriet to treat you nicely if you call, but you'll have to raise your voice or she won't understand what you're saying."

She asked me to get Harriet from the kitchen.

I walked down the hall into the kitchen where Harriet was busy chopping vegetables. There was a big stockpot simmering on the old six burner stove. The aroma of something delicious was in the air. Harriet interrupted my reverie and yelled at me, "That was too long!"

"I'm sorry. Miss Edith wants to see you."

"What?"

I repeated it a little louder.

As we started into the sitting room, she shouted so Miss Edith could hear, "Don't let it happen again!"

Upon entering the sitting room, Miss Edith raised her voice, "Harriet, Arthur will be coming back from time to time. He's welcome. I want you to be friendly."

Harriet scowled. "I'll try," she said in a low voice.

Harriet frowned at me. I was happy she had put down the knife.

It seemed like time for me to go. Miss Edith was exhausted. I thanked her for the time we'd spent together and told her I'd be in touch soon.

Harriet showed me to the door and slammed it behind me. Don't take it personally, I thought. After all, she is hard of hearing. So far I seemed to be an expert at more than financial planning around here. Around here, I was the guy who could make people cry and be angry.

Miss Edith had given me an idea. If the older Butler son had told his younger brother that he was leaving town a century ago, there would never have been a murder. Now in a parallel universe, I needed to break the chain of events.

I headed back to the Lancaster home. Like the people in town, I didn't want to call it the Butler house anymore. It was time for history to rest in peace. The financial plan had to be acceptable to the Lancaster clan to stop the murder.

The Parlor

My visit with Miss Edith had calmed me down and helped me focus. The house or ghost meant me no harm. Why I had accepted this case in the first place started to make sense. Throughout the initial phone call, my instinct was to turn JJ down. There was a third parallel going back almost forty years ago. At that time I worked as a sales engineer. The South Georgia business I was calling on was owned by a father and two sons. They had an invention that required products that I sold. I had expected an equipment order from them. After a dead zone of two to three weeks with no communications, I found out one of the twin sons was dead and the other son was in jail. The company was in another part of South Georgia, but on the other side of the state. The invention was sold off to a competitor by the father. It wasn't the loss of business that bothered me, but the loss of three good people that I enjoyed working with. Evidently forces stronger than myself had compelled me to come help JJ and his family.

CHAPTER EIGHT

JJ waited for me on the porch. Sarah Jane must have sent him outside. He had a cigar in his mouth. He motioned me to sit down. When I chose a chair upwind from him, he laughed. "What did you do in town?" I lied, telling him about doing a walking tour of the historic part of town. My answer shouldn't have made any sense to him but he accepted it.

After some more pleasantries, which I'm not good at, I said, "JJ, you ever think about having a marketing representative call on various commodity brokers in the big Southeast and Gulf of Mexico ports? You know, relying on the computer with no personal touch may come back to haunt you when the big corporations compete with you."

"I don't get your drift." JJ seemed puzzled and sucked on his cigar.

I hoped my short story left him wondering but the vagueness drew him in. I had to approach this quietly. This had to become his idea.

"When the big guys need to crank up commodities because sales fall off, they'll hire marketing people to go wine and dine the brokers to buy their cotton, not yours. What are you going to do with all that cotton if no one buys it?"

"Do you know something I should know?" He puffed on his cigar, gazing at me with narrowed eyes.

"No, my job with my clients is to try to stay ahead of what's going on. I advise clients on their investment strategies. Commodities are a volatile item. Another possibility is the big boys will start buying up all the cheap land again since economy is picking up. If your competition thinks they can sell more cotton, they'll need more land. That'll drive land prices up. You won't be able to make those sweet land deals anymore. Then they'll have to sell the cotton." This was a convoluted statement, but it got his interest.

He tapped the ash off his cigar into the big old amber glass ashtray and stared at me with a worried look. I was at best a rank amateur around commodities, but it didn't take a detective to figure out that with the economy improving, land prices would increase.

"What should I do?"

"Well, maybe you ought to consider hiring someone to make personal calls on the many brokers you deal with. Now is the time while you still have the assets and cash flow. The right marketing person can help boost your future sales significantly."

I tried to put some urgency in my voice. Did he take the bait? He was sucking on the cigar clamped in his mouth so hard the tip was glowing like a steel furnace. I sat quietly in my chair. I watched his face change as his mind worked over the seed I planted.

"JJ, why don't you try the idea out on your sons tonight to see what they think?"

"Good idea, Arthur. These get-togethers can be boring for me."

Gotcha. People trust me because I mainly sell ideas, not products. There was no monetary value to me if he hired a marketing person. He blew a smoke ring and looked skyward. If there was a time to shut up, it was now.

"JJ, I'm going to freshen up before dinner."

Ken Zahn

He nodded his head and continued puffing some more. His rocker was rocking at a steady pace and I thought he looked relieved to have a new idea about his business operations to consider.

I went into the house and climbed the stairs, squelching a growing feeling of apprehension. What would I find in my room? The yellow glow from the afternoon sun was warming the room. That removed the dread. Trying to relax, I sat in the easy chair and watched the sun set over the fields. There was nothing else to do for the moment. I thought about JJ's father starting a legacy that was in the process of being destroyed because of antiquated notions about "blood" and "first born" rights of inheritances. "Just like the town," I thought. A strong sense of foreboding about Robert and John again invaded my mind. There was danger awaiting this family. My visit with Edith Faircloth had only intensified it. Somehow, I had to help them avoid disaster. The first step was planting the thought of hiring a marketing representative with JJ. "We'll see how dinner goes," I mused.

Soon there was the noise of people arriving, I washed up, put a clean shirt on and went downstairs. Robert and his family had arrived.

Robert introduced me to his wife, Susan, and son, Robert Jr., known as "Bobby." Robert said he was six, but he looked maybe 7 or 8. I am not good at little kid's ages. Bobby hid behind Susan's skirt. He was a cute little boy. Susan was pretty, not beautiful, with a pleasant voice and easy manner. I knew why JJ and Sarah Jane liked her. Eager to show Bobby off, Robert took his hand and asked me to go outside with them. JJ followed me out the door.

Robert had brought a small football. He and Bobby tossed it back and forth. The little kid was good. When Bobby made a diving catch, I clapped and yelled and JJ joined in. Robert beamed. He was a good father.

Soon, John arrived with Cindy. He walked around and helped her out of the car. Robert kept on throwing the ball to Bobby. Cindy could turn a man's head from a block away. As she approached us, I could see that she wore too much makeup. Her dress was out of fashion. On the other hand, she was wearing high heels and too much jewelry for an informal get-together. In this little town she was a queen.

The Parlor

What did she know about me and my purpose in being there? No doubt, she was going to be cautious about what she said regarding family matters. John stiffly introduced us. Cindy turned on the charm, complete with a soft Southern accent, sparkling eyes and a big smile. "It's so nice to meet you." With that out of the way, Cindy turned her attention to Robert and Bobby who were still tossing the ball around. "Hi there!" Bobby dropped the ball and came running up to give her a big hug. "Aunt Cindy!" She wrapped her arms around him and just beamed at all the men around her. *God, she was like a spider, just working on pulling the next Lancaster heir into her web.* I wasn't sure if she was giving me chills or the air had suddenly turned cooler. Robert stood there tossing the ball from one hand to the other. Thankfully, JJ clasped his arms around his sons and led us all into the house. It was getting dark.

For phase one of my plan to work, JJ had to be alone with his two sons. Then he would blab about hiring a marketing person. As I entered the parlor I saw Susan go into the kitchen to help Sarah Jane. Moving quickly, I sat down near Cindy. John was off fixing her a Diet Coke. I didn't know much about her. What was the easiest question to get her talking? No problem here. "Cindy, what sorority did you pledge at the University?" Pay dirt. When John heard her start on that monologue, he moved over with his father and Robert. Cindy was talking so loudly I couldn't hear JJ, but I could see John and Robert staring at him.

Just from their expression I could tell that JJ was telling them about hiring a marketing person to call on commodity brokers. They were silent and caught off guard. They just continued to stare at him. His business decisions affected their job function. When he had puffed hard on that cigar, he was considering the suggestion.

After the long sorority story, Cindy took a long drink of the Diet Coke. Phase two began. "After the glamour of University life, living in this town has to be depressing. The clothing in the window of the dress shop looks like it's been there since the 1980s. Don't you miss the shopping malls in the big cities or the charm of towns like Charleston?"

Ken Zahn

Just as John was depressed about his office, I gambled that Cindy would be depressed at the local shopping opportunities.

Cindy's face went serious but she laughed. "Yes. I do. I feel isolated here. The local stores have such a low turnover and they buy the cheapest clothing. I have trouble buying clothing on the web. They never seem to fit right. Arthur, I know this dress is out of fashion and I realize I wear too much jewelry." She almost sounded human.

The response was perfect for the next line of questions.

"Do you go shopping in Atlanta, Charleston or Savannah? Or are they too hard to get to?"

Cindy smiled. "I do visit my sorority sisters occasionally. They all live in big cities where I can shop. I really enjoy those trips. But it is still hard to get in much shopping with all the other social activities, especially for clothing."

Good. The power of suggestion had worked. It was almost too easy. I had one more thought for Cindy before dinner. This might be my last chance to talk to her alone.

"I understand that JJ and Sarah Jane bought you and John a historic house and Sarah Jane restored it. If it's anything like this house, it must be beautiful."

Cindy responded, "I never would have chosen the house myself. The rooms are small. You should see the kitchen. There's almost no counter space. Having houseguests is difficult when my friends visit from time to time. It's hard to entertain. I really would like a new house with larger rooms."

My timing was perfect. We'd gotten to where I wanted to be when I saw John coming back. Would John tell her what JJ had just said about needing a marketing representative on the coast? I wouldn't know until after dinner. Sarah Jane called us to the table. The seating chart had me sitting at the opposite end of the table from Cindy, but she was sitting next to John.

We sat at a table for eight. The table looked elegant, but the meal was simple fare. We had baked chicken and a number of vegetable dishes. Cinnamon told me that we'd have peaches for dessert. Sarah

Jane was definitely concerned about JJ's eating habits. Somehow the conversation drifted around to my two murder cases. Because Cindy was listening, the real truth blew up a notch or two. Under normal circumstances, the two cases bring back morbid details and I shut off any requests to talk about what had happened.

I told them that I'd been invited to speak around the country at black tie affairs, meeting important and beautiful people. It was one big fat lie. I can spin a yarn when I need to.

After dinner Cindy watched me, looking for her chance. Just before the evening ended, she motioned to me when no one was looking.

"Arthur, is this true?"

"You mean about me meeting beautiful people?" I tried to keep her off-guard.

"No, about JJ considering hiring a marketing representative." She was interested. From what John said, she made the decisions for them.

"I suggested he consider it." The tone was casual and low keyed.

"Who does he have in mind?" She wasn't going to let this go.

"It's too early to say, but probably someone based on the coast that would travel to all the coastal towns, maybe also to Atlanta and Charlotte or even possibly New York." I laid it on. No holding back now. Time was running out.

"Oh!" Cindy went back to join John. He was talking to his father. John wouldn't have a choice once Cindy began working on him. JJ and Sarah Jane would agree if John volunteered, but it had to happen quickly.

I regretted not spending any time earlier with Susan, but she had busied herself helping Sarah Jane and Cinnamon fix the meal and she also sat at the other end of the dining room table. Now she was sitting alone. Robert and Bobby were talking to Sarah Jane. I sat down next to Susan on the sofa. "Your son is a cute kid. "

She laughed. "He's the best thing that's ever happened to us."

That wasn't good news to my ears. There was no mention of marriage to Robert. With that, she looked over at Cindy with an appraising glance. "Robert, it's time to go. Bobby has a special Cub Scout outing in the morning."

Ken Zahn

That was the clue for everyone to say good night and take their leave.

The house went quiet. Cinnamon cleaned up in the kitchen and Sarah Jane straightened up the parlor. JJ and Sarah Jane said they were dead tired. I decided to be a good house guest and said good night after complementing them on a lovely evening with their family.

Before going downstairs, I had left lights on in my bedroom. Otherwise, it was dark upstairs. It still was a long time to my normal bedtime. I sat in the easy chair, replaying the day's events. Cindy would have to burn John's ears tonight; there was still time. JJ had no plans to visit the Lancaster office tomorrow. John would either have to come to the house or call if he wanted to talk to his dad.

Not wanting to waste the remaining hours of the day, I began scratching up a financial plan that might work. My planning is done the old fashioned way, by hand. By midnight it was done and it was in my computer. The plan was complete with graphics. It only took three to four hours to complete, which was normal. JJ had a printer to print the document. JJ also had an all important shredder. All my scratched-up notes could be shredded. Satisfied – a bit smug even – I wondered what could I do next? I was afraid to go to sleep.

I moved to the desk chair. The desk chair had been very uncomfortable. Would sitting in that chair keep me awake? Being really wound up plus the uncomfortable chair seemed like the answer. But eventually I slipped into slumber anyway while sitting in the chair. The chair couldn't overcome a sleepy wave that oozed through the walls of the room.

CHAPTER NINE

With a jerk of my head, I jolted wide awake. As I sat there for a moment, my ears were listening and my brain was wondering what woke me up. All old houses make their own night music. The room was cool. The lights were still on. I must have been really exhausted to have dozed off while sitting in the uncomfortable wooden chair. That's why I sat in it. I had wanted to stay awake. It was 3 a.m.

I stood up and stretched. I was dressed in an old sweat shirt, pants, and shoes with socks, but I could still feel the coldness of the floor. After visiting the bathroom, I sat down in the easy chair to think. How to pass the time until morning? I don't know why but all of a sudden I had to make it look like I had slept in the bed. I decided to rumple the covers and sheets.

As I pulled the bed covers back a shiny, bright red spot glistened on the pillow. Stupidly, I touched the spot to see if it was wet. A flash of light shot through my brain. The flash of a gun shot. Was that what had awakened me? Upset, concerned, worried thoughts were pulsing through me. Vague remnants of a dream came back to me. I had dreamt of being in this room asleep until I heard the noise and smelled the odor of a gun going off. Death was closer.

Embarrassed, I tried to try to clean up the wet spot by carefully removing the pillowcase. The spot was so fresh it hadn't even penetrated to the pillow. I took it to the bathroom sink to try to get the spot out. *Use some cold water* came to mind. Rinsing the spot with cold water and soap faded it, but didn't get it out. Still embarrassed about the spot, I knew I had to say something to Cinnamon.

This was the second night that I hadn't slept well. It is possible for me to keep going on four or five hours of sleep for a day or two, but then I crash. Tomorrow, actually today, was a key planning meeting with JJ and Sarah Jane. Could I keep my energy level up? If my stamina faded, I might not be able to continue and a death could follow. Wide awake now, I sat back in the hard wooden chair. Even if I wanted to sleep, no way I would lie down on that bed.

The house was dead silent. It had spun a web around me. I wanted to leave, but there was only one way to do that – my financial plan for JJ and Sarah Jane was the key. In addition, each son had to feel like he'd gotten the best deal. To stay awake, I fired up my computer and reviewed my thoughts, making some adjustments to the plan.

What was the worst that could happen? Robert would kill John. Then JJ and Sarah Jane would lose both sons. I couldn't let that happen.

I reviewed the plan again. John was not the problem. But Cindy had to push John to take the marketing position. Would the plan satisfy Robert? Yes, if John left town. There was nothing more to do; the plan was saved and the computer shut down.

Sitting there, I knew neither the house nor the ghost meant to harm me. The entity, whatever it was, needed my help. Very tired now, *just how gutsy are you* came to mind. I couldn't lie on the bed; that was too much. Sitting in the easy chair would put me to sleep. I moved the wooden desk chair near the window. I got an extra blanket out of the chest of drawers and turned off the lights. My eyes adjusted to the dark. There wasn't much of a moon that night so I could see a sky full of stars. I hadn't watched the heavens in a long time. City lights, smog and the business of day-to-day living had erased the night sky from my mind and sight. The moonlight was just enough to let me see the fields stretching behind the house.

Seeing the stars had encouraged me. Like old friends, they would never abandon me.

On that dark, windless night the silent house was frozen in time.

The next thing I knew, the room temperature was dropping like a rock. I crossed my arms over my chest to keep warm. As it got colder and colder, I tightened my arms around myself until I was like a mother hugging a baby. Now I was shaking. Was it because I was freezing or because I was terrified?

A mist filled the air until the far side of the room disappeared. In the mist, the image of a person formed. Was this a dream? Was I awake? The image, although faint, was illuminated by the moonlight, and sharpened as it came closer. No matter how hard I tried, I couldn't move.

It was an elderly man in a long night shirt. His unkempt hair was long and wispy. His face was unshaven and gaunt. He seemed to be 85 or so. No smile. He held a shining object. Damn, it must be the gun. I was still trying to get up, but nothing would move.

He was saying something over and over. Finally, I made out the words.

"I'm sorry, I'm sorry."

Then as quick as a blink of an eye, the room returned to normal. Sweating, I was a mess, mentally and physically. Hoping to gain some comfort from gazing at the stars, I looked out the window. Dawn was approaching, the stars had faded. Did I faint? Did I nod off? All I knew was that it was very early in the morning.

As I went into the bathroom, the faint light from the bedroom revealed an image in the bathroom mirror. It wasn't me. I quickly turned the light on and it disappeared. Spooked and shaking, I took a hot shower and dressed. The spotted pillowcase was hanging over a towel bar in the bathroom, just as I had left it. Touching it again, it felt dry already, so I took it into the bedroom. When I went to put the pillowcase back on the pillow, the blood spot was gone. Holy crap! This was driving me crazy! Never before had any paranormal events affected me.

Ken Zahn

Before I left the room I checked to make sure the bed looked slept in and that the spot was gone. I needed to get out of the house. A long walk would do me good.

The sun was barely up. Going down the stairs, I heard someone come in the back door. My heart skipped a beat. I stopped on the stairs when I heard clattering in the kitchen and knew it must be Cinnamon.

As I entered the kitchen, I could see Cinnamon with a bowl of strawberries in one hand and a container of half-and-half in the other. She closed the refrigerator door with her foot. Pale early morning sun came through the window. I was so happy to see a real person, a person I knew. She wasn't wasting any time. She was starting breakfast preparations. What could be more normal then that? My eyes took it in. She saw me looking at her. Her first words were: "Mr. Arthur, you've seen the ghost." Not, "You look like you've seen a ghost." She knew. This was bewildering to my mind.

"Cinnamon, you know something."

"I know not to sleep in that room in this house. I know you've been to see Miss Edith."

"How do you know about Miss Edith?"

"It's a small town. Harriet told me. She and I have been friends for a long time."

"What do you know about that room?"

She took coffee mugs, bowls and plates out of an upper cabinet and began to set the table as she talked to me.

"I only go in there on a bright sunny day. I change all the beds in the house every week or so. Sarah Jane wants to be ready for any unexpected guests... Sometimes there's blood on the pillowcase in that bedroom. When I can't get it out, the pillowcase gets burned at my home. Miss Sarah wonders why we run out of pillowcases so fast."

"There was a blood spot on the pillowcase last night, Cinnamon."

A plate slipped through her fingers and crashed to the floor. She was frightened. We picked up the pieces. After a minute or so, she said she felt better.

"Has anyone else seen it?" I already knew the answer.

The Parlor

"John did. He told me. It about scared him half-to-death. It started after Robert beat up John in college. Then right after college John got married and didn't stay in the house. The spotting stopped. But it started again before you came. This is serious. Are you all right?"

"Yes." But it was a lie. "What do you know about the mirror in the bathroom?"

She had to sit down. She told me Sarah Jane found the mirror in the attic. She liked the frame. She had a new mirror inserted and put it in the powder room. Soon no one wanted to use the powder room and people commented about the mirror. The ladies especially complained that their appearance seemed aged. One man came out white as a sheet and has never returned to the house. Eventually, it ended up in that bedroom, which is rarely used. I have seen what it can do. I turn the light on before I enter the bathroom. I never go in there in the dark. Then she said, "You've been visited by the spirit of the house, whoever or whatever it is. It's trying to tell you something."

"Yes, the spirit spoke to me. I think I understand the words."

"This has gone further than any other occurrence. I'm scared for you, Arthur."

"I'm OK, but I need time alone to think. A long walk will do me good."

The solution had come to me earlier in the shower. Robert had to be confronted. I'd do the planning with JJ and Sarah Jane, but before day's end the issue with Robert had to be settled.

Walking in the morning calm through the fields, the sweet smell of earth surrounded me. I've often felt I was born at least a hundred years too late. To have come to this country and been the first to have tilled the land must been a great excitement.

As I returned, JJ stood on the back step, watching me. The long walk put some color back in my face.

"It was a wonderful time to take a walk." He rolled his eyes. The land was all business to JJ. Too bad. We went in.

Ken Zahn

As JJ opened the back door of the house, I thought of New Orleans and the French market. The delicious smell of freshly brewed chicory flavored coffee hit my nose. Breakfast won't be at all bad if we have delicious hot coffee. Surely Sarah Jane wouldn't deny me jam for my toast?

Sarah Jane was in the kitchen with Cinnamon. She said, "Arthur, you should have taken JJ with you. A long walk would be good for him."

JJ rolled his eyes again. Could he keep up with me? I walk at about a mile in fifteen minutes. In the past hour, I had walked about four miles. With JJ's heart, it might have been too much for him. What would I do if he had a heart attack?

Sarah Jane asked me about my plans for the day. "Sarah Jane, you and JJ are going to have a full day with me. Like it or not, we'll have a plan outlined by the time the sun goes down."

She stared at me. JJ looked straight at her. "He's supposed to be quick, Sarah Jane. He had all night to think about the plan."

JJ had no idea how close he was to the truth. Yesterday I had worked on Cindy; today I'd tackle Sarah Jane. If Sarah Jane agreed, JJ would fall in line.

Family chatter at the kitchen table was the way to start the day. Bobby with his kiddy football was the big topic. Sarah Jane commented how proud she was of Robert as a father. But she didn't say as a husband. JJ recounted some of his own memories of throwing the ball around with the boys. We covered every family member except Cindy.

After three cups of strong coffee, I was ready to start. We went into the parlor, much as I dreaded it. This is where it all <u>began</u>, 150 years ago. Would it <u>end</u> somehow in the parlor? A concerned look covered Sarah Jane's face as we entered the parlor. She was kept in the dark about JJ's financial affairs. Considering that, the conversation would have to start with Sarah Jane. If she understood the plan and felt it benefited everyone, I could proceed to the twins. JJ wouldn't be an issue. Treat the financial plan like Sarah Jane treated her house. If the pieces made sense and were in order, she would accept it. We started with her family history.

"Sarah Jane, tell me about your mother and father. What was the cause of death for each of them?"

"Arthur, this is hard to talk about. I loved them so much."

"I'm trying to estimate your life expectancy."

"Oh, I'm in perfect health." Everyone says that.

JJ pitched in. "Sarah Jane, answer his question."

Sarah Jane looked at JJ, and then sighed. In a subdued voice, she replied, "My father was an alcoholic. He died of liver disease. He spent almost everything he earned on Crown Royal whiskey. My mother denied herself food but made sure my brother and I got enough to eat. After my father died, she worked odd jobs to keep us going. Her health was poor. She died while I was at the UGA at age 38."

"What about your brother?"

"He inherited my father's love of liquor. He killed himself in a car accident, while driving drunk."

"So that's why you don't allow liquor in the house."

"Yes. I still worry about the boys."

"Are there any signs of problems?"

"Not that we know of, but we do know that they both did drink at Georgia. Here in town, we don't know. We do know Cindy hides a bottle at the house, but we don't think John drinks."

"What about Robert?"

"He's the one we worry about."

Frankly, from a financial planning perspective, this was qualitative information that would never be found in a financial planning fact finder. There never would be a line to fill out as to whether a family member was alcholoic. Cindy's alcoholic temptation might be important, but it would be important find out about Robert. If his parents worry about him, then maybe they know the answer. But for now, Sarah Jane's potential life expectancy still needed to be determined. My planning was based on her living twenty to thirty years.

"Sarah Jane, do you have living relatives who might have remembered the War Between the States?"

JJ choked on his coffee and had a coughing fit. Sarah Jane laughed. Pay dirt. For the next hour or so, she went over her family tree. And what a tree! She had plenty of life expectancy. She took very good care of herself. She told me she was 60. JJ rolled his eyes a few times, but he was defenseless. He had to wait her out.

"What do you think, Arthur? Come on now, tell the truth."

She smiled.

"You'll make the morning Today Show birthday greetings for people who live past 100."

After JJ stopped laughing, Sarah Jane asked. "Is life expectancy that important?"

"From a planning perspective, it sure is."

It was time for a short lecture about how family wealth should be spent. Family wealth should benefit clients, not their children or grandchildren. Her lifestyle was an objective of the plan. She nodded. JJ was dead meat and he knew it. I had something in mind, and he knew he couldn't wiggle out. The plan must allow Sarah Jane to maintain her house and lifestyle. That was that. At the moment she was clueless about where the money came from. My plan would show her where her income would come from if he died. That was the key.

As soon as I finished with Sarah Jane's health and family history, JJ knew what was coming next.

"JJ, fess up to Sarah Jane about your health."

He was stripped bare. Sarah Jane stared at him. He sputtered. Before he could speak, Sarah Jane spoke.

"I knew when JJ asked you to come here that it was for more than planning for the boys and the company's future. It was because JJ was scared. He's worried about me, too. He hates to have people tell him what to do. Arthur, I know that's what you're going to do."

"That's what he hired me to do, but I need your help. This plan has to be right for both of you."

This exchange bought JJ a few minutes. "Go ahead, tell her."

JJ told her the truth. That he needed a major operation, and he might not make it through it. The doctors wanted to operate as soon as possible. He had sought a second opinion, but the diagnosis was the same.

She cried. She might have already known all this, but it was hard to hear the truth.

Sarah Jane needed a few minutes to compose herself before we went on. "JJ, what did your doctors say about your life expectancy if the operation was successful?"

"I could live for another ten to twenty years, but they wouldn't know for certain until after the operation."

Even JJ teared up. He and Sarah Jane were struggling to compose themselves. It can be really uncomfortable when I help clients face the truth about their financial and health circumstances. I'm not a touchy feely kind of guy and I have just learned to wait it out quietly. We were still working through the emotions, when we heard Cinnamon speaking to someone in the kitchen. We looked at each other.

Ken Zahn

As far as I knew, no one was expected, but we heard Cinnamon laughing. John came through the back hall into the parlor. "Oh, John! This is a surprise!" Sarah Jane got up and hugged him, then said she needed to freshen up and would be back. "Mom, what's wrong?" He gave JJ and me a quizzical look. John never came to the house during the day. Phase one and two from last night had worked. Cindy had talked to him last night. John knew we were meeting and he couldn't wait to hear the financial plan; Cindy gave him no choice. What he would say was critical.

CHAPTER ELEVEN

John looked scared, tense. He knew we were in a private meeting. JJ had no idea why John had come. He was irritated. Everyone was silent for a moment. "John, we were just breaking for lunch. Would you like to have lunch with us?" I asked.

I could see JJ staring at me, but I ignored him. John's arrival was perfect timing. His parents' reaction was pivotal. The first part of my plan appeared to be working. Only time would tell.

He nodded yes. "Tell Cinnamon to set another place for you," I responded. When he left and before JJ could speak, I put my hand up to quiet him. "JJ, he has something to say. It's important. Be pleasant. Get that frown off your face. Ask him about cotton futures to loosen him up. You've already put him on edge." Hopefully, his kitchen task would calm his nerves.

Sarah Jane came back, and I told her what I had told JJ. She nodded and wagged her finger at JJ. "Let's go into the kitchen." In the kitchen, Sarah Jane hugged John and then began to help Cinnamon. JJ did what I had told him to. Soon John and his father were discussing business and John looked comfortable. This wasn't going to be easy. John was here about the marketing position. Could he broach the subject? He wasn't going to leave until he asked for the position. I would make sure of that. This was a key planning issue.

Lunch was a subdued family affair with Sarah Jane rambling on about how much she enjoyed dinner last night. While the three Lancasters talked, I waited my turn.

Thank God for the Internet. I had logged on after breakfast and checked out the overnight business news. Finally, a lull in the conversation gave me a chance to jump in.

"JJ, I heard you and John talking about cotton futures. This whole commodity situation is affecting all investors. Apparently, foreign investors can't make up their minds about what to do. They're bailing out of contracts today." JJ was tense. He nodded. He went through these up and down markets every day.

This was John's opportunity to tell JJ why he was there. No response yet. I prodded JJ to keep the conversation going.

"JJ, if prices don't rebound that's going to lower the value of your land, how much Uncle Sam will get, and my fee."

They all laughed. John had better strike now. Lunch was over. Sarah Jane and JJ wanted to get back to their planning.

JJ was moving his chair back when John finally spoke up.

"Dad, were you serious about hiring a marketing representative to call on commodity brokers in the Southeastern ports?"

"Actually, Arthur brought it up. It might be a good idea. What do you think, Arthur?"

"Well, JJ, you're big enough to seriously consider getting your name out there, considering the volatile market situation."

No way was I going to let this die. I looked at John. "You must have something on your mind." This was why Robert had played quarterback on the high school team and John hadn't and was the best choice to run the company if and when JJ died. John looked at me and finally he started talking.

John went into a long, thoughtful monologue. He really wasn't that busy. John confessed to what JJ already told me, that staff people did most of the work. John thought that Robert, with the help of both staffs and the computer, could do the day-to-day company operations. Small town living really wasn't his and Cindy's style after living at the University. Finally, he got it out. Would JJ consider him for the marketing position? He emphasized that he knew more than anyone else they could hire, and that he always had the interests of the company in mind when he had to negotiate. "Dad, this is a family legacy. I promise if you give me this chance, I'll make you and Grandpa proud."

Listening to John was like listening to my conversation with Cindy last night. She had primed him.

JJ looked at Sarah Jane; she had tears in her eyes. I had to wind this up, but Sarah Jane took over.

"John, you're not planning to move away permanently? You would keep the house here?" Sarah Jane spoke softly.

"We'd come back every few weeks or so," John reassured her. "I still want to be active in the business, but Robert would run the day-to-day affairs."

Sarah Jane calmed down and smiled. JJ was stunned. He needed to speak. This discussion was on the edge. It could go either way. I kicked him under the table. His head shot up. I am sure no one ever did that to him. But he understood.

"John, I definitely would consider you the best person for the job. I can trust you in a way I can't trust any other person. Let me talk further about this with your mother and Arthur, but I am sure it will be OK." JJ was biting his lip, doing his best to keep his emotions under control. He coughed and pulled out a hankie. "Damn cigars give me a fit sometimes." They also gave him an excuse to wipe his eyes and blow his nose.

John beamed. He'd done the hardest thing he had ever done in his life. Maybe Cindy proposed to him, rather than him to her? He didn't have to worry about a job after college, like the rest of us. Cinnamon cleared up the dishes. She smiled at me when no one was watching. She knew this could stop the blood spots. She would help me. I could trust her.

When Sarah Jane walked arm in arm with John to the door, JJ said "Damn, Arthur, you planned that, didn't you? I can't believe this. This is going to cost me, isn't it? Now, what about Robert? "

JJ was a smart old fox but I had outfoxed him. He wasn't mad.

Sarah Jane came back with a smile on her face. She would miss her son day-to-day, but she was glad Cindy wouldn't be around to stir up mischief. She told JJ to work this out with me. There was a big period at the end of her sentence. She wanted her son to be happy.

Would all this work out? It still depended on JJ's operation and Robert's cooperation. My planning had to work whether JJ survived the operation or died. It had to be simple. JJ had confessed that the doctors wanted to do the procedure soon.

Happiness flooded my brain. Now the financial plan would make more sense. Day-to-day office tension would disappear. We went back into the parlor. It was going to be the beginning of the end. The plan will satisfy them.

CHAPTER TWELVE

The morning energized Sarah Jane and JJ. Their anxiety over the planning, John's turnabout, his proposition and lunch shifted them into high gear. I asked Cinnamon for strong black coffee and told her we weren't to be disturbed. She nodded. She had her serious face. She was pulling for me. In her heart, she knew what the blood spots meant. These two boys were part of her life.

My financial plan may be as short as one or two pages, even for a multimillion dollar client. A long plan may be five to seven pages long. The one for Sarah Jane and JJ ran seven pages. I knew it wouldn't take long to present. I had made copies on JJ's printer. Each had a copy so that they could follow along with my presentation.

"First thing, I like to have you review and confirm that this is a correct listing of all the information you shared with me."

JJ and Sarah Jane looked it over. He nodded. She seemed surprised at the large financial numbers but nodded as well.

I explained to Sarah Jane and JJ that there were probably a dozen techniques I could use. The one proposed could be implemented quickly. It would give them flexibility no matter what happened. The technique isn't well known to the public and probably rarely used. It's called a "recap" in financial planning slang. It's a stock recapitalization where the company issues preferred stock in exchange for the client's common stock. Keeping my explanation simple, I started with something JJ had done when his father died.

"JJ, you told me that when your father died, you forced the government to use a lower value for the land because of the bargain basement purchases you had made prior to his death."

He smiled.

"Well, we're going to force them into agreeing to our value for Lancaster, Inc. with what I'm proposing."

Part of the agreement to accept JJ as a client required him to give me a value for the Lancaster stock. Based on that, I was suggesting that some of JJ's stock would be re-issued as preferred cumulative paying a substantial dividend. The IRS regulations state that the size of the dividend established the value of the preferred. The higher the dividend, the more the preferred stock would be worth.

Attempting to not move too quickly, I explained what a dividend was to Sarah Jane. I made it sound like interest on an investment. The investment was the Lancaster stock. I could see she understood because of what she said next.

She laughed. "JJ, you are going to have to part with more of the cash you have hidden away,"

At first JJ didn't like the idea of the corporation paying a dividend. "Listen, Arthur, I need cash on hand for land deals. I don't want to be paying any dividends."

"Hear him out, JJ. You brought him all the way up here to help us." She was coming on strong.

Confident, I went on. "This accomplishes four goals. First, it freezes the value of the stock in your estate at the preferred stock value based on the dividend. Second, it provides income to you if living and income to Sarah Jane if you die. Third, the preferred is issued with voting rights. This gives the owner control of the corporation. Fourth, along with the remainder of the plan, it will force the government to make a decision on the value of Lancaster stock because of the gifting issues."

She had to be able to follow me. Looking at her, she didn't look concerned.

"Sarah Jane, let me explain what would happen if JJ dies first. The value of the preferred stock never increases. That's why it's called a freezing technique. The federal government never shares in the growth of the corporation. You get income for the rest of your life, and you would control the company with voting rights."

I let that sink in for a moment while I drank some coffee. We went to page three. From here on we would mainly be addressing the Lancaster stock issues and rather than dollars, the plan used percentages. She nodded in agreement.

"I'm going to have your attorney issue you preferred stock equal to 75 percent of the corporation's value. Then the remaining common stock represents 25 percent of the value of the company. Again, 75 percent of the value of the company would be preferred and 25 percent would be common stock." I realized I was repeating myself, but this was a critical starting point.

JJ looked puzzled. Sarah Jane sat quietly. "JJ, this is a paper transaction created by the attorney. No taxes of any kind will have to be paid. There may be a fee to Georgia for issuing the preferred, but it will be minimal. JJ will still own 100 percent of Lancaster." The plan could be explained in minutes, so I had to slow myself down.

"The next two pages assume JJ's operation is a success and he lives for another 10 to 20 years."

JJ smiled and Sarah Jane held his hand. JJ waved me on. He was on edge. Who wouldn't be when you were talking about their death?

Ken Zahn

"My second planning technique is also not well known to the public. It's called a charitable stock bailout. You would give 10 percent of your common stock to the University of Georgia. It would be an outright gift and would allow you to take a charitable deduction. It provides you with a huge current cashless income tax deduction. This will force the IRS to either accept the value of the gift or make an adjustment to the value. It doesn't matter what they do, and the University's lawyers would do most of the battling to make the value as high as possible. This would help cement the value of the preferred stock. The common stock value and the preferred stock value cannot exceed 100 percent of the value of the company. Later, the University would sell the shares back to the corporation, not to you. There couldn't be a formal or informal agreement that the University would sell the stock for redemption or that it would be redeemed. It's called an unrelated redemption but, frankly, the University will redeem the stock at some future date. When the University redeems the stock the corporation would have to have liquidity or make a loan to buy the stock back."

JJ groaned, but I went on. He hated to part with cash. Now I raised my hand and asked him to be patient.

I moved slowly, making sure they understood each step. That's why I used simple percentages, not dollar amounts.

"When the University redeems the stock, it would substantially reduce the value of the corporation's retained earnings or its estate value. Then the remaining common stock initially valued at 25 percent could be squeezed down to 15 percent. Remember, you have already gifted 10 percent to the University. That's when you gift the 12 percent of the common stock to your sons at a reduced fair market value. Each would get 6 percent. You may have to pay a gift tax, but that also reduces the size of your estate further and you get a credit at death. The actual dollar calculations are on the last page, but the estate and income tax savings are substantial."

We went back to the percentages again. "We may be able to get the gift value to your sons down further by issuing the common stock as non-voting and paying no dividend. I'll work with your CPA to get you every discount possible on the gift of the stock to your sons. You or Sarah Jane will still control the corporation. Most of the future growth would be transferred to your sons when they own the common shares." I stopped for a moment. Through experience, I knew it is important to give clients time to read over what they just heard described. That way, we all stay on the same page going forward. We were discussing upper level estate planning in a very simple presentation.

The forth page was a graphic flow chart that illustrated how the plan would work. At the top it said "JJ lives 10-20 years." JJ and Sarah Jane continued to review the chart with me until they were satisfied.

By having the third page spell out what was happening on the fourth page of the flow chart, they could follow the chart point by point. They asked a few questions. Sarah Jane made notes on the flow chart. Actually, when clients make simple notes on my flow charts, they understand them. There was a lot of planning on one of my pages. JJ looked at Sarah Jane. She smiled and held his hand again. She was satisfied so far. JJ asked about the 3 percent and I said I would cover that later.

88

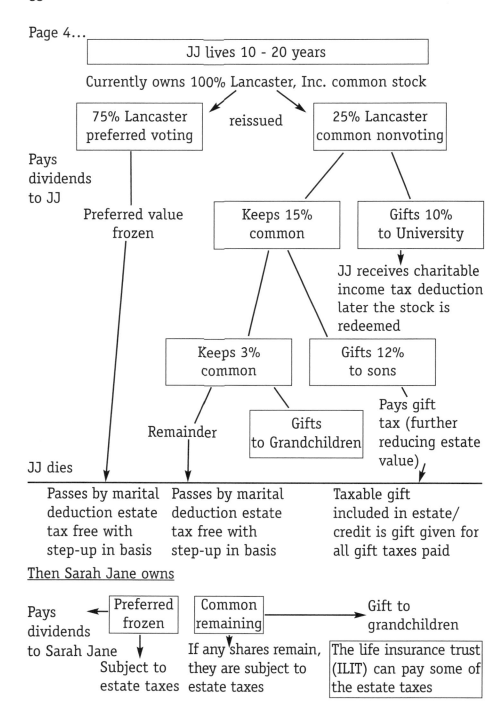

| JJ lives 10 - 20 years |

Currently owns 100% Lancaster, Inc. common stock

75% Lancaster preferred voting ← reissued → 25% Lancaster common nonvoting

Pays dividends to JJ

Preferred value frozen

Keeps 15% common

Gifts 10% to University

JJ receives charitable income tax deduction later the stock is redeemed

Keeps 3% common

Gifts 12% to sons

Pays gift tax (further reducing estate value)

Remainder

Gifts to Grandchildren

JJ dies

Passes by marital deduction estate tax free with step-up in basis

Passes by marital deduction estate tax free with step-up in basis

Taxable gift included in estate/ credit is gift given for all gift taxes paid

Then Sarah Jane owns

Pays dividends to Sarah Jane ← Preferred frozen

Common remaining → Gift to grandchildren

Subject to estate taxes

If any shares remain, they are subject to estate taxes

The life insurance trust (ILIT) can pay some of the estate taxes

JJ asked, "Where's the bad news chart?"

Page 5, the bad news summary and page 6, its flow chart, came next. Actually, they started the same as the prior pages by reissuing the stock. I explained the major difference was a passage more by estate tax laws than income tax laws. Since the preferred would be valued when the attorney does the reissue, the stock would get a step-up in basis at JJ's death. Sarah Jane would still get the 75 percent preferred stock and the 3 percent common stock. She would control the company. The preferred and 3 percent common stock would pass by the marital deduction. The IRS could argue about the value of the preferred, but the preferred affected the value of the common.

I tried to emphasize the difference in how the plan would work if JJ died earlier.

Just like the prior flow chart, the 25 percent consisting of common shares would be split. Ten percent would be left to the University, 12 percent to the sons, and 3 percent to Sarah Jane. JJ's attorney or CPA could try to get the value of all the stock reduced by arguing that he was a key employee and also that the common stock was unmarketable because it was non-voting. The 10 percent to the University at JJ's death would reduce the value of the taxable estate and because that will be a charitable gift, the remaining shares that would go to the sons could be discounted further. There would be an estate tax due, but at both a reduced rate of 35% and at a substantially reduced value. Just like the prior chart, there still would be an estate tax due at Sarah Jane's death. It could be reduced by the exemption amount. Then I talked about the uncertainty of the estate tax law. I said I was hopeful the exemption might be at least $5 million, but who knew twenty or more years into the future.

90

Page 6...

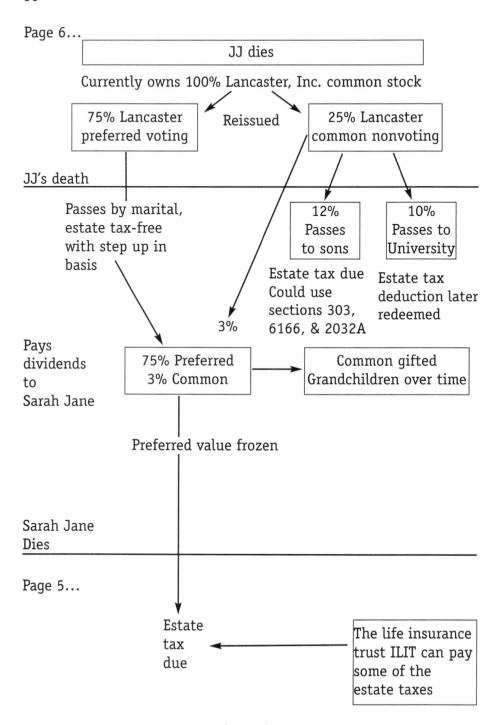

JJ dies

Currently owns 100% Lancaster, Inc. common stock

75% Lancaster preferred voting   Reissued   25% Lancaster common nonvoting

JJ's death

Passes by marital, estate tax-free with step up in basis

12% Passes to sons

10% Passes to University

Estate tax due Could use sections 303, 6166, & 2032A

Estate tax deduction later redeemed

3%

Pays dividends to Sarah Jane

75% Preferred 3% Common   →   Common gifted Grandchildren over time

Preferred value frozen

Sarah Jane Dies

Page 5...

Estate tax due   ←   The life insurance trust ILIT can pay some of the estate taxes

The Parlor

On the seventh page I summarized both charts simply:

1. Either way, JJ or Sarah Jane would end up with preferred dividend paying stock. The stock would have voting rights (control).

2. A portion of the common stock would be either gifted to the University (JJ lives) or left to the University (JJ dies) to reduce the value of the remaining common shares.

3. The remaining common shares would go to their sons either by gift (JJ lives) or inheritance (JJ dies). The value of the common stock would be discounted so that either gift taxes or estate taxes would be substantially reduced.

4. At Sarah Jane's death, presuming she died second in both cases, the life insurance in the Irrevocable Life Insurance Trust (ILIT) would help pay estate taxes.

I explained that I had no idea of what the estate exemption amount (the tax-free portion) might be many years into the future. More discussion followed, but they seemed to accept and understand. JJ liked my plan because he would maintain control, make a non-cash charitable gift to the University, and reduce gift or estate taxes down to a minimum.

The actual calculation now included the value of the house, personal property including collectibles, and other investments. The size of the estate tax grew substantially. JJ reviewed the actual numbers and the tax savings. All he said was, "That much?"

He didn't say how many dollars were saved or how many dollars still needed to be paid in taxes. "JJ, it would be worse if we didn't transfer the common stock to the University and your sons. This is the worst financial case."

I eased the burden slightly by saying his attorney or CPA may also be able to apply three IRS code sections which could help provide estate tax liquidity (Sections 303 and 6166) and an estate tax discount (Section 2032A). I handed JJ some printed material on these code sections, but did not explain them. I had brought the material with me because I knew they could apply.

"Do you have any additional suggestions?" JJ asked.

Ken Zahn

"Yes. We are going to apply for more life insurance, but it will only be on Sarah Jane's life. It will provide more estate tax liquidity. In addition, I have some more planning techniques to use after your operation. You will see me some more."

JJ liked the words "some more." He seemed satisfied.

Sarah Jane liked the plan because she would get a substantial income for life. She hadn't known where her income would come from after JJ's death. That concern went back to her family's hand-to-mouth existence. They both liked knowing that the growth of the business would be in their sons' hands, not subject to estate taxes.

JJ was wearing down, but not me. "Are you finished?" he asked. He looked exhausted.

"No." They both looked at me with puzzled expressions.

JJ said, "What else?"

"There are some hidden ideas on the flow charts. I'm concerned about John's marriage. I like the idea of him being the marketing arm of Lancaster, but the bright city lights may charm Cindy. Right now John doesn't own any stock. Once John owns the stock, Cindy could get rights to those shares if she outlives or divorces him. I am not an expert on Georgia law; that's why we will need your attorney's opinion."

They looked at each other. Now it was JJ who was squeezing Sarah Jane's hand. JJ hadn't thought about this next level of planning, but I had.

"As part of this planning, your attorney will draw up a comprehensive buy-sell agreement between your two sons. Even Bobby will be kept in mind in the document. You wouldn't want Cindy owning half of Lancaster, would you?"

"You just made me feel a lot better Arthur. You had me really worried," JJ said.

The next part was touchy. I was in uncertain waters. "As part of the plan, JJ will announce that he or Sarah Jane will be retaining a 3 percent interest in the common non-voting stock. Part of that 3 percent would be gifted yearly, using the annual gift exclusion, to your grandchild and all future grandchildren."

"I don't get this," JJ said.

"Many years ago, the Congress passed the kiddie tax law. The IRS taxes children on unearned income at the parent's marginal tax rate above certain levels. Since this common stock will not pay a dividend, there will be no income until it's redeemed, let's say for college. The stock would grow tax free until that time. On the optimistic side, the stock could be worth $400,000 to $600,000 in 10 years or more when Bobby goes to UGA. There would be some capital gain tax to be paid, but the stock would be out of your estates. "

"Ok, Arthur," said JJ. "Please continue."

"This would allow you to make yearly cashless gifts using the common stock. Sarah Jane could continue to gift to your grandchildren after your death."

Neither picked up on the word "grandchildren". I baited Sarah Jane. "Sarah Jane, would you like more grandchildren?"

Her face lit up. "I'd like a little granddaughter or two since I had two boys. Robert and Susan have told us they plan to have another child or two. Cindy might even decide to settle down and become a mom. I know John wants children. And if I had a whole brood of grandchildren to spoil, that would be just fine with me."

JJ was thinking money, not grandchildren.

"Where would the money come from to pay the preferred dividend?" JJ asked.

"From a combination of company profit and reducing your salary."

"WHAT?" Sarah Jane was still holding on to JJ's hand. It was almost as if she knew what I was going to say. There had been one concession after another from JJ. Sarah Jane nodded for me to go on. She was enjoying herself. This was making sense to her.

"I have another computer run that shows you reducing your salary. This reduces federal and state income taxes, and reduces Medicare taxes plus the upcoming health care tax. Unfortunately, to accumulate the money to pay the dividend, Lancaster will have to pay substantially higher taxes."

The money look was back in his eyes.

"JJ, issuing the preferred is easy. I will have to work with your CPA on how to structure the dividend. But with computers, we can do that in a matter of hours. Remember, we're talking about many types of taxes: estate tax, gift tax, personal income tax both federal and state, and corporate income tax. Also, there are income tax limits on gifts to charities and charitable gifts can trigger the alternative minimum tax. The trade-off is to achieve the greatest tax reduction. In this case, the trade-off is higher corporate income taxes. But the bottom line is that the dividend may ultimately retain its 'qualified dividend status.' If the law stands, the dividend you will receive could be taxed at 15 percent."

JJ reviewed this carefully. I kept going back to the fact that the final result was that he paid more corporate taxes but less personal taxes. When you also add state taxes, the calculation can get more complicated. He saw how this all fit together. "The good news is that Sarah Jane could get this income for life from Lancaster. There are a lot of trade-offs. The plan isn't perfect. The major savings is in estate taxes, but the gift to the University while living reduces income taxes. The corporate tax to pay the dividend is the big negative."

"How long will it take to implement this plan?"

"This plan and calculations need to be reviewed by your attorney and CPA. First, you must agree to the planning. They will need some time to review it. I'll have to push them along. If this is acceptable, the attorney can split the stock into preferred and common fairly quickly. Valuing the preferred with your CPA will take time, but the plan works either way."

I used "either way" because I hated to say, "JJ, if you die on the operating table, it works."

"The future of taxes is uncertain, but this plan gives you the flexibility you need to avoid paying excessive estate taxes. In addition, the existing life insurance and new life insurance on Sarah Jane fit perfectly into the plan when the bulk of the estate taxes will be due. And Sarah Jane will be guaranteed income for life."

Sarah Jane said, "JJ and I will discuss this. I want this settled."

That was that. There was more that could be done to save taxes, but I needed to get this planning in place first. Then I could come back and we could do more planning. With the lack of sleep and the emotions of the planning details, I was exhausted. But Sarah Jane had saved me throughout with her firmness.

CHAPTER THIRTEEN

Sarah Jane and JJ were also exhausted by all this discussion and decision making. They needed a break to discuss this. My next issue was Robert. Leaving the house, I decided to go back to see the Sheriff. Were there any records on the murder in the house? I called for Miss Edith, and Harriet answered. "Come by in an hour." Cinnamon must have said something to Harriet. It's a small town.

At the Sheriff's office, the receptionist motioned to me to go back to his private office. It was getting too easy. This time the Sheriff was awake. He laughed. "Solved the murder yet?"

I laughed. "Yes." This was getting contagious.

He nearly swallowed his tongue. He coughed, wheezed, snorted and blurted out, "Say what? Come on, Arthur."

"Miss Edith knows who the murderer was. Her grandmother was engaged to the murdered son. I'm meeting with her in an hour. She'll confirm what she knows."

"Can I announce that the murder's been solved?"

"Nothing can be proved. It's all conjecture and hearsay. I know in my heart who murdered the son. I'd like to pin down some more details and I can use your help."

"Ask away," the Sheriff said.

"I'm still searching for any records from the time of the murder. Did the former Sheriff hide anything? Anything at the old building that housed the newspaper?"

"Sorry, there's nothing. If anyone has anything, it's Miss Edith. She really is confiding in you, isn't she? Amazing. I wish I could be there with you."

"This has to remain between Miss Edith and me for the time being."

"She will call me, won't she? I would love to just be able to talk to a lady who I remember was the height of Southern charm and beauty."

"She will. And Sheriff, I may also need some other help."

"What kind?"

"Quiet police work."

"You want me to keep something quiet?"

"You may have to, but it won't be illegal."

"Anyone but you would get locked up for asking me this, but the Florida Sheriff said to trust you. Sometimes you work outside the law. Is that the situation?"

"No, there's nothing yet, but I'll let you know."

The Sheriff asked me about the Florida murder case I had been involved in.

Since I had some time to spare before my appointment with Miss Edith, I settled back in my chair and relived what had happened. I can tell a good story when I want to. He was all ears. He laughed and waved his arms in wonderment. He especially enjoyed the part about Gibby, the son of the Florida murder victim, stepping on the toy trains and falling down with a house shattering thud. Anyone who has stepped on sharp metal toys in their bare feet knows the pain it causes. I described the brawl between the Sheriff's deputy and Gibby at the house, and me putting Gibby out of action with gun shots before he could beat me up.

"You really did that? You shot but didn't kill him because you knew he wasn't the killer? Lord have mercy, what I wouldn't give for a case like that." He was grinning.

The Parlor

"No, you wouldn't want a case like that. Three people died." He stopped grinning and nodded his head.

As we walked toward the front door I told him I'd get back to him after I saw Miss. Edith. I waved at the receptionist on my way out and she waved and smiled. She must have heard the Sheriff laughing. I had entertained the Sheriff on yet another boring day. Both of the times I had been in his office, the telephone never rang and there were never any other officers around. Now I was in her good graces.

Outside, the bright sun totally blinded me. As I stood there for a moment while my eyes were adjusting, a car stopped in front of the office, cutting me off. A young person got out and ran around the car. As soon as my eyes adjusted, I could see it was Robert. I said, "Oh, hi, Robert. How..."

He was in a foul mood. He yelled, "So John-boy gets invited to lunch and I don't. Does he run the company now?"

Caught off guard, I wasn't ready to take him on. My mouth was open but nothing came out. He got louder and more offensive by the minute. He was literally in my face. I remembered that he had beaten up John so severely that he had to be hospitalized. He got between me and the Sheriff's office. There was no place to go. Unlike the Florida case, there was no gun and he didn't need one.

I thought quickly. "Robert, calm down. No decisions have been made that affect you or John."

That was a lie, but trying to explain the sophisticated planning out on the street to a raving person was next to impossible. What I could say would do no good. It could make it worse. He stepped forward and started poking me in the chest. I stepped back. His car kept me from falling. "You're going to tell me right now..."

The door to the Sheriff's office flew open and the Sheriff charged out, hand on his gun. He knew what was up, but kept his cool. He gripped Robert's shoulder and quietly told him to back up and shut up. The Sheriff was bigger than Robert and looked stronger.

"Robert, go home, take a cold shower and cool off. If I see you at Arthur's throat again, I'll throw you in jail no matter who you are. You hear me?"

Ken Zahn

After a pause, Robert got in the car and started to drive away. The Sheriff was watching him. Then he said, "You and I aren't done yet, Arthur." I went inside immediately. No telling what he would have done if the Sheriff hadn't come out.

The receptionist looked concerned. She must have seen and heard everything. I asked her what her name was. "Nancy," she replied. I smiled.

"Are you OK?" she asked.

"A little shaken up, but I'm fine," I reassured her.

Once Robert had driven away, the Sheriff came back in. "Come back into my office. I think you'd better give me an explanation of what just went on."

Before we started, he poured us both a cup of execrable coffee and told me to come clean. He was concerned because he had just taken on JJ's son. "What the hell was that all about?"

"Sheriff, I'm going to tell you a story you won't believe but Miss Edith will confirm." I told him about the ghost, the blood, Cinnamon confirming the blood spot and my belief that the murderer was the Butlers' second son. The ghost was the spirit of the second son. It was trying to get me to stop Robert from killing John. Strange as it sounded, I felt like I was living in the past and the present at the same time.

The hairs stood up on his arms. He believed me. He said that the prior Sheriff had a paranormal experience in a murder case. Strange things happen in these old houses. He asked what he could do.

"There's no evidence against Robert and no crime has been committed. The answer to stopping a murder is within me. Sarah Jane and JJ will probably agree to a financial plan later today. Robert has to be satisfied in order to end this. If the ghost disappears, then I'll know there'll be no murder."

"What happens if you can't satisfy Robert?"

"Then I'll call you. I swear, if I feel Robert will do harm, you will be called."

"Lordy, this is better than the Florida case, isn't it?" The Sheriff grinned.

"Yes, but only if I can stop the murder. You and Miss Edith are the only people who will know. That set-to outside your office needs to be kept quiet."

"Nancy hears a lot, but she won't say anything. This is the nothing part you mentioned I need to be quiet about, isn't it?"

"Miss Edith will be calling you in about thirty minutes. She'll be short and to the point. I better get going."

At Miss Edith's house, Harriet opened the door and actually said hello and smiled at me. Did I want some sweet tea? "Two glasses."

Entering Miss Edith's sitting room, she said, "It's close, isn't it, Arthur?"

Holy crap, I thought. Had she heard what happened in town? No, she was asking about sleeping in the murder room. I told her all that had happened. It seemed like weeks were going by, but it was just a day. She knew about the blood spot from Harriet, who had heard about it from Cinnamon.

She hadn't heard about the face-off with Robert in front of the Sheriff's office. There was fear in her eyes.

"Robert's going to act soon."

"Yes."

Harriet brought my sweet tea. I chugged one glass down to the last drop. I told Miss Edith the Sheriff knew that the house was telling me there had been a murder in the past, and there could be another soon. The Sheriff would help us.

"You're certain you want him to know?"

"Robert was right on the edge of losing it. The Sheriff saved me. He needs to know you believe me. If I need to call for help, he'll come right away. Please give the Sheriff a call to confirm all this."

"Alright, if you are sure? Here's the phone. Get him for me." Nancy put him on the line immediately. Miss Edith briefly talked to him and blushed before hanging up.

"What did he say?"

"None of your business, Arthur," she answered with a Mona Lisa smile. I could imagine what she must have looked like to an admirer years ago. Enough of this, Miss Edith had to help me. What would Robert respond to after the incident at the Sheriff's office?

Ken Zahn

"Miss Edith, do you have any idea how I should approach Robert?"

"Did Sarah Jane and JJ decide whether to do the financial planning?"

"We're almost ready to proceed. All I have to do is to get their attorney and CPA to agree to the plan. The implementation will be done by them."

"I realize you cannot discuss the planning, but how will it affect Robert?"

The question jolted me into action. The Robert issue had to be settled today. I told Miss Edith I had to make a telephone call. I called JJ. Cinnamon answered. She asked me how Miss Edith was. After answering, I asked to talk to JJ. When he came to the phone, he asked me where I was. "In town. What time is dinner?" He said Cinnamon could have answered that question. He sounded cranky. I told him he needed a nap. JJ replied grumpily, "What's up?" He didn't appreciate my sense of humor.

"Have you heard from Robert today?" Was Robert keeping out of sight?

He avoided the answer. "Sarah Jane and I feel John will get what he wants, but we're still uncertain about Robert."

They'd been discussing the plan. Perfect, we were nearer a conclusion. An opening to Robert was on the table.

"Invite Robert for dinner and tell him he has to stay the night," I instructed JJ.

"Why? He only lives 10 minutes away." My request caught JJ off guard.

"If you want this to be solved by breakfast, he stays the night."

"You're sure? This is strange."

"Invite no one else, and don't take no for an answer." I was firm.

JJ moaned a little, but agreed. "Arthur, you are the most peculiar person I have ever met."

After I hung up the phone, Miss Edith nodded at me. She knew what I was going to do. When Robert and I went upstairs for the night, he wouldn't go to his old bedroom. He would be forced to sleep in John's old bedroom. The ghost needed to be flushed out.

"Do you think this will work?"

"For one thing, the only person he can murder tonight is me, not John. I can explain the plan in detail to show him how he'll benefit. The ghost has to cooperate."

"How will you know it worked?"

"If I survive the night and Robert accepts the planning. The next night I'll sleep in the bed."

Miss Edith hesitated. "Where will you be while Robert is sleeping in the bed?"

"I'll be in the room, sitting in the easy chair."

"This won't be easy, will it?" She looked at me sympathetically.

"No. Do you have any other ideas?"

"Yes. I'll pray for your soul. I know you're trying to do the right thing and no one can help you."

"I'll call you tomorrow. If anything happens to me, you should tell the Sheriff everything I told you. He will do the right thing. He's a good man."

Maybe the night would pass without any deaths, especially mine. Miss Edith was wrong when she said no one could help me. She had helped me by letting me talk this out. What would I have done if I hadn't met her? I made a mistake coming alone. This wasn't a financial planning case; this was a murder mystery story.

Ken Zahn

Traveling from Miss Edith's house back to Sarah Jane and JJ's house gave me time to think. I wanted to ask Cinnamon some questions and to also ask for her help. Luckily JJ wasn't waiting for me on the porch. His spies must have missed my face-off with Robert. Entering quietly, I went into the kitchen. Cinnamon was busy prepping for dinner.

"Arthur, let me look at you," she said.

"You've heard what went on in town with Robert haven't you? JJ hasn't heard about it, has he?"

"Right, Arthur, this is a small town."

"But how..."

She smiled. "I have better sources of information than he does."

Was Sherman's March through Georgia watched as closely as my activities? Cinnamon would have to help me. The events of the evening had to appear to happen naturally. I sat on the corner stool and watched as she continued preparing chicken for the oven.

As soon as she finished, I asked, "Is Robert coming tonight?"

"There was a major argument between JJ and Robert on the telephone. But he is coming." Cinnamon picked up a wooden spoon and began stirring the collard greens on the stove. The aroma of the kitchen was making me hungry.

"I want Robert to have to sleep in my room, not his old room."

When she heard that, Cinnamon put the spoon down and looked directly at me. A concerned look came across her face.

"Are you going to make him sleep in the bed?" she said, concerned and wild eyed.

"Yes, unless he wants to sleep on the floor. Is his old room ready and the bed made up?"

"Sarah Jane asked me to get the room ready for him."

"Well, don't tell anyone. Strip the bed clean. No towels, not even toilet paper in the room. The same with the other bedrooms upstairs, I want them barren. In my room, put one roll of toilet paper, two towels and washcloths and leave the bed made up."

"Sarah Jane will be very unhappy." A frown creased her forehead. She asked what I was up to.

"Cinnamon, you need to trust me. Sarah Jane will never know about it. What happened in town gives me an advantage over Robert."

"If Miss Edith trusts you, I trust you," she said, a bit reluctantly. "What do you think will happen?"

"If all goes right, the ghost will be satisfied and finally rest in peace."

"How will you know?"

"I'll sleep in the bed tomorrow night. Where are JJ and Sarah Jane?"

"Resting. JJ wore himself out getting Robert to come here tonight. He and Sarah Jane discussed family issues for a long time after you left."

"I'm going to clean up for dinner."

"Are you OK?" Cinnamon asked me.

"No, but I'd better recover quickly. This is the final episode. It's all over one way or another tonight."

Cinnamon waved at me with her wooden spoon. "Let me be now, or there won't be any dinner tonight or any stripped rooms."

Ken Zahn

The warm glow of the setting sun hit me when I opened the bedroom door. It encouraged me to fight through this, as strange and unsettling as it was. I had no idea what would happen or how I'd make it happen over the next twelve hours. Dealing with a ghost was a first for me. Normally, as an outside consultant, I stayed away from emotional cases like divorces, remarriages, business break-ups, and family arguments. They were too stressful for me. I was sitting in the chair by the window; my mind was blank. There was no other choice than to convince Robert that my financial plan would work for his benefit. If that didn't work, make him sleep in the bed and hope the ghost could convince him. This was the craziest case I would ever encounter.

I'd left the door to the hallway ajar. I faintly heard JJ talking to Cinnamon downstairs. Time to start the next phase.

Leaving, my eyes were blinded by a flash of sunlight off a shiny object. Was this really happening or was it a function of something planted in my brain? Nearly falling to the floor, my body was barely able to stand upright. In this semi-conscious state, a name floated into my brain, "Edith."

Was the ghost, with great effort because it was daylight, trying to help me? But what did Edith's name mean? I pulled myself upright.

Walking through the house, I tried to calm myself and think. JJ sat in the parlor. As I entered, JJ said, "Arthur, you look like you've seen a ghost."

People kept saying that. It wore me down and left me on edge.

He laughed, I didn't. At least he was in a good mood. He added, "Getting Robert to come tonight wasn't too bad, but getting him to stay the night was like the battle of Atlanta. It nearly turned into a bloody mess. You're sure this is the solution?"

"Yes." Nodding my head, I shifted the conversation. "I'm sure you and Sarah Jane have discussed the plan. What do you think?" I was trying to shake my emotional state by getting back to business.

"I hate to pay those Beltway people any more than I have to, but I see you're trying to minimize it. What is important is whether it can be implemented quickly. I haven't been feeling too well. Maybe I'm worrying about the operation."

The Parlor

"What does Sarah Jane think?"

"She likes your plan because she knows as long as Lancaster exists, she'll be in control. She loves her sons, but she doesn't want to answer to them."

I thought to myself that in all my planning cases, no parent wants to give up control to their children. They want to run their lives to the very end. With Sarah Jane's family history, the planning fit her.

"We can start things moving right away. Are you ready to do this?"

"Yes, what are you going to do?"

"I'll send the plan and calculations to your attorney and CPA tonight so we can get their opinions tomorrow. The rest can be handled over the telephone from my own office over the next few days. It won't be necessary to go to Atlanta."

"I feel better already. I need to call my doctor as soon as possible. They want to get me on their surgery schedule."

With so few pages, the plan sounded simple to JJ. Actually it wasn't. I had a battle on my hands tomorrow to get the attorney to act quickly. This was uncertain ground.

Just about then Sarah Jane came in wearing a lovely summer dress and beaming. No question, she'd support me and make decisions. JJ's health had clouded his ability to make decisions. She was in control.

"You have a good afternoon, Arthur?"

"Yes." Wow, what a lie.

"What have you been doing in town?" She was interested in how I'd been spending my time when I disappeared.

A second flash hit me. Was this really the ghost or my subconscious trying to help me think? Luckily, I was sitting down. When I didn't say anything, she said, "Are you all right? You look like you've seen a ghost."

JJ laughed again. Finally, after composing myself, I replied, "I'll tell you at dinner." Robert needed to be there when I told the Miss Edith story. All of a sudden, my thoughts came together.

Before anything further could be said, we could hear Cinnamon greeting Robert in the kitchen. Sarah Jane got up. "I'll get us some tea. Robert can help me carry it in." JJ looked at me rather forlornly. He needed help.

"JJ, let me handle the planning issues." The afternoon discussions with Sarah Jane and the confrontation with Robert on the phone had exhausted him. His health might also be affecting him.

When Robert came in the parlor, he was nervous. His reluctance to come into the house was based on what had happened in town and his father's pressure to stay the night. JJ normally had a laid-back relationship with his sons.

Robert sat quietly on the sofa and didn't participate in the small talk. He wasn't sure why JJ had summoned him. He must have hoped his parents hadn't heard about his dust-up with me. It was time to open the can of worms.

"Before dinner's ready, I think we ought to tell Robert what's up while we're here in the parlor." Why not do it in the parlor? Hopefully, it would end here.

Sarah Jane piped up, "Yes. We want to get this settled." She was already stepping up as the family matriarch. I thought to myself, no matter what happened with JJ's surgery, she'd be okay.

Robert looked startled and sat up straight. Sarah Jane continued. "If we talk at the table, Cinnamon will know our business. No need for that. People will know soon enough."

"Yeah, I think it would be better to do it now rather than spoil the finger lickin' good dinner." Everyone laughed, including Robert, and the tension in the air was gone. It was the right moment.

"OK, JJ, tell Robert about your health."

"Shoot, Arthur, I thought you would lead off."

"No, tell him." I was insistent.

JJ laid it out. He was to have a serious operation and he might die on the operating table. If he survived, he'd have a shortened life expectancy. He stopped there, but I looked at him and pointed to myself. Then he said, "That's why Arthur is here. His job is to find a way to keep the company out of the hands of the IRS."

What he didn't say was it was also to keep his two sons from killing each other. JJ finished and then said, "Are you going to show him the planning?"

"Yes." I proceeded to go over the planning, but, frankly, it was all beyond Robert. He didn't understand corporations, charitable giving or taxes. Freezing the value of the preferred stock, the majority interest, was beyond his scope of knowledge. He was focusing on the 6 percent he and John would each get. This had to be simple and to the point. "Robert, all the future growth of the company will be in your hands."

But Sarah Jane saved me. She said with a firm voice, "Robert, listen up. JJ and I aren't going to just give you the company. You're going to have to work for it. It's our family's company and it should benefit all of us."

Her stern voice startled Robert. It was time to drop the other shoe. I said, "Robert, John was not invited to lunch yesterday. He just showed up."

Robert finally spoke, but not with the curbside defiance from earlier in the day. If he had shown that now, Sarah Jane would have disinherited him.

"What did John want?" he asked.

"He wants the marketing job. He's willing to turn the day-to-day company operations over to you."

"You mean he's willing to leave town?"

"No, not permanently," Sarah Jane interjected quickly and with a bit of concern. "He'll come back to review company operations and visit periodically."

Robert had better be careful. Dealing with his mother was on new ground. She was speaking as if she were in control. He saw his question had offended his mother and backtracked, realizing that would be a bad card to play.

"I didn't mean it that way, Mom."

Overcome by all of this, Robert realized his entire life was about to change. Cinnamon saved us by announcing that dinner was being served.

We were all hungry and focused on the meal. There were no rolls, no butter, no gravy, but the baked chicken was deliciously spiced. I even had a second helping of collard greens. Cinnamon knew how to

Ken Zahn

cook. The talk was small talk. Sarah Jane asked about Susan and Bobby. After the coffee and sugar-free donuts were served, time to tell my story. "Before you arrived, your parents asked me what I've been doing in town these last few days."

His head jolted back, the donut clattering onto his plate. He looked worried. The conversation had gotten his attention.

I explained that the house's pedigree and history had intrigued me. Through the Sheriff, I found out that Miss Edith Faircloth knew a lot about the house and the Butler family. I had gone to see her. My story surprised everyone.

"You actually saw Miss Edith?" JJ blurted.

"Yes, twice."

"Arthur, do you realize men my age had eyes for her even though she was 20 or 30 years older? Did she tell you how old she was?"

"Are you serious? You don't ask a lady her age," Sarah Jane exclaimed.

"Yes, the Sheriff told me the same thing about her." JJ smiled. "Miss Edith's grandmother was engaged to the oldest son, who died in this house. Her grandmother told her about the family history, the history of this house, and life during and after the War Between the States."

"Did you know that Confederate soldiers were recruited in the parlor? Did you write all this down?" Sarah Jane said in a stunned voice.

"Well, no."

"I've asked Miss Edith to our United Daughters of the Confederacy meetings for years. She won't come to the house."

"I doubt she ever will. But it's possible she'll see you."

"No one has seen Miss Edith in years," JJ said, "and you walk into town and see her twice. Amazing. How's she feeling?"

"She had a terrible case of skin cancer, but she's pretty feisty for her age. Harriet watches over her."

Cinnamon was listening as she cleared the table. "You really get along with Harriet?" JJ asked.

"Yes." JJ looked at me and rolled his eyes. He knew Cinnamon and Harriet were old friends.

Sarah Jane was enchanted with all this. "Does she know what happened in the house that night?" she asked.

"Her grandmother told her that the younger boy killed his older brother. But you must understand that her grandmother was engaged to the older son and the way Miss Edith tells it, the younger son also wanted to marry Miss Edith's grandmother." That was key information for tonight's bedroom story for Robert. She was sitting on the edge of her chair. "You will get an e-mail next week with everything I know."

"This story would make a great novel," Sarah Jane commented.

Robert looked uneasy. This was hitting a little too close to home for him.

Cinnamon told Sarah Jane she'd be leaving shortly. She gave me a thumbs up as we left to go into the parlor. Robert's room was stripped bare, along with all the others upstairs except for mine.

In the parlor, JJ took his son aside to go over the plan and outline the business operations. Sarah Jane sat close to me.

"You're amazing! You know more about this house than you let on." I smiled enigmatically.

"Is it at all possible that Miss Edith would see me and allow me to record her story?" she went on.

"Probably. I'll ask her, but she won't come to the house. She's very self-conscious about her appearance. She might see you at her place." The truth was she wouldn't come to the house because of what had occurred.

"What JJ said about Miss Edith was true. Every young girl wanted to look and act like that regal lady. There was just something about her."

"There must have been."

"She is the last tie I know of to the days of the old Confederacy. There are few people alive today that reach back 150 or more years. I believe you when you said she heard about it from her grandmother. Miss Edith is one of the few remaining who know about the sacrifices, the deaths and the aftermath directly and not from a book. I hope she'll share those memories with me. Sorry, Arthur, but this is more exciting than the planning."

I revealed that if everything worked out, I'd try to arrange it. "Wonderful." She beamed.

Ken Zahn

The evening was winding down. I looked across the room and saw Robert and JJ. They were animated but somewhat quiet. It was starting to sink in for Robert that his parents really did want the best for the family and the business. Finally, JJ and Sarah Jane said good night and retired to their room. Robert and I were alone.

There's an old saying, "He who speaks first loses." I buttoned my mouth and in a few moments Robert finally spoke up. "I guess I'll go to bed. I'm exhausted."

Nodding my head, I remained seated like a stone statue. He needed to go upstairs first before I went upstairs. It had to be pitch dark downstairs.

After Robert left, I turned off all the lights downstairs. The light coming from the upstairs bedroom gave me just enough light to see by. JJ and Sarah Jane's room was downstairs, off to the side of the kitchen. A faint crack of light filtered under the door. I wanted to make it as hard as possible for Robert to see his way to get any bedding. This was it. I'd done everything that one could humanly do. Now the ghost needed to do his part.

CHAPTER FIFTEEN

By the time I climbed to the top of the stairs, Robert had gone to his room and discovered that everything down to the soap was gone. Wildly, he charged down the hall towards me.

"My room is stripped bare! I don't even have toilet paper. What's going on? Cinnamon never messes up. This your doing, Arthur?" He was suspicious.

"Yep." Boy, that was to the point. He stepped back.

"What?" He exclaimed, obviously not happy.

"I want you to be in my room all night."

"What?" Robert's temper was beginning to boil.

"You've either seen or felt the ghost in the house, haven't you?" I hit back hard and fast.

"You're as wacky as Miss Edith. She put you up to this." But he never answered my question.

"No, Miss Edith had nothing to do with it. I've had two appearances of the ghost in two nights."

"You're not making sense!" He waved his arms with a look of sheer panic.

Robert was irritated and getting louder. Standing in the hall was not the way to settle this. I quickly went into the bedroom; he continued to stand in the hall. "Do you have the nerve to stay in this room tonight?" The challenge came to him from inside the room.

He didn't move. The ghost had bothered John because he had slept in the room. Then the blood spot had appeared prior to my arrival. Did Robert know something? Robert remained motionless. I closed the door. After a few minutes the door opened. He peered in.

"I think you're a crackpot. Where do I sleep?" he asked. It was still early evening and he couldn't leave the house. Robert had promised his father that he would stay the night. His mother's attitude had stunned him tonight.

"In the bed, of course."

"OK, where are you sleeping?"

"In the easy chair by the window."

"Cinnamon left an extra towel and washcloth for you in the bathroom but I don't have extras of anything else. There is no extra soap or toilet paper."

Looking ill at ease, he slowly proceeded into the room. I was already sitting in the easy chair near the window. He came across the room slowly and sat down in the hard desk chair across from me.

"Why are you doing this?"

"In the morning I'll tell you or you'll know why. But in the meantime I'd like to talk to you about running the company." He nodded his head. That was OK.

"My concern is about firing key personnel. You will need them and their expertise when John leaves town. It might also affect your father's health if long-term employees were fired. Where would they find another job? Lancaster is the town's main source of revenue." We talked this out for awhile. I thought my reasons made sense, but Robert didn't agree.

The Parlor

"We'd be more profitable!"

"Look at the company's financials; the bottom line is that Lancaster is always profitable even in bad times. Robert, do you want to be known as Scrooge around this town?"

"No."

"Do you need more money?"

"I'd like a nicer office."

"That's easy enough. I can arrange that with your father."

We talked, or mainly I talked. As the night progressed, I intentionally got more boring and began repeating myself. It got late. He was wearing down. I could sleep in my chair but doubted he could sleep in his. His eyes blinked. I rolled on about employee relationships, profitability, financial ratios, blah, blah, blah. Finally it was too much. Robert went into the bathroom to change into his pajamas. If he had come out in a 1850s night-shirt, my jaw would have dropped. But no, he was in his pajamas when he came out and got into bed. The only light remaining on was a small room light near the easy chair. Robert looked exhausted. Maybe he would be asleep in ten to fifteen minutes. I quietly entered the bathroom and just sat on the toilet with the seat down after I changed my clothes and brushed my teeth. Time passed. I turned off the bathroom light before leaving. There was no reflection in the mirror. It was totally dark in the bathroom. Quietly, I opened the door. He was asleep. The floor creaked as I tip-toed, turning off the room light before reaching the easy chair. He didn't saying anything. It was out of my hands.

The stars shone brightly on a moonless night. I prayed that all the right decisions had been made. All that one-sided conversation exhausted me. Soon I was soundly asleep.

I had been asleep for what seemed a long time when a quiet moaning filled the air. The sound came from Robert. Was this a dream? I pinched myself hard enough to hurt. The room was frigid, and the windows had fogged. The ghost – or what appeared to be a ghost – hovered over the bed, uttering something. The strange sound was like wind blowing through a crevice. Robert wasn't moving but his moans were increasing. I wouldn't help him or wake him. He was fighting

Ken Zahn

the ghost. Both sounds – his and the ghost's – got louder. The room temperature dropped another ten degrees. What sounded like a shot from an old pistol rang out suddenly.

Robert leaped out of bed. He must have seen the murder. He ran towards the light switch but plowed into the door. The room was cold, foggy and dark. The impact knocked him down. When he recovered, he got up and turned on the lights. I was still sitting in the chair. His face was bloody, but not from running into the door. He looked horrified when he saw the pool of blood on his pillow. I still said nothing. He ran into the bathroom without turning on its light. He was out in a flash.

He yelled at me, "Did you see and hear all of that?"

"No, but I have seen it over the past two nights."

I guessed he had just seen the argument in the parlor, the ghost saying he was sorry, then the murder and now the reflection in the mirror.

Robert was sweating profusely even though the room was still cold. He came and sat across from me. "Arthur, help me out here…" If there was any chance to convince him to not murder his brother, it was now. I told him what I had found out from the Sheriff and Miss Edith. He listened intently.

"I'm seeing a parallel between what happened here 150 years ago and today. You have so much anger I believe you could kill your brother. The ghost feels it and has transmitted it to me over the past two nights."

"What's the ghost saying?" Robert asked.

"The ghost is trying to tell you he's sorry he killed his brother. He could have used his brother's help running the plantation. Killing his brother shortened his father's life and drove his brother's girlfriend into another man's arms, not his."

Robert nodded. Robert saw the parallel. It wasn't identical, but close enough.

"You've been thinking about John having a 'fatal accident' haven't you? Then you could run the company." It was a guess, but worth a try.

The Parlor

He quietly answered, "Yes."

"Robert you're getting what you want. You'll run the company. Your brother will handle the marketing and will phase out quickly. Let's hope JJ survives the operation. He'll need bed rest for awhile and if you have temper tantrums, you'll kill your father. He'll want to rely on you. You have to be a good quarterback and throw soft passes to your brother. He can help you. Growing the company and marketing go hand and hand. Give him a chance." He just nodded at me. The room had warmed up. He asked, "What about the blood?"

"It's gone from your face and the pillow. Go look. There will just be one small spot left."

He looked and nodded his head. He did turn the light on in the bathroom before he entered. He dressed quickly without saying a word. "I'm out of here." In minutes, he was gone. Did he accept or even understand what I had just said?

With a deep sigh, I slumped into my chair. Was this the end? Had I stopped the murder? The sun was visible over the horizon. Finally it was time to take a hot shower and go down to breakfast. It was going to be a long, hard day with JJ's advisers. I would have to use up what remained of my energy.

Ken Zahn

It was still very early as I walked down the stairs. Cinnamon was preparing breakfast in the kitchen. JJ and Sarah Jane were still in their bedroom. Without a "good morning," she asked, "What happened?"

"I will tell you what you need to know. You can't tell Harriet. I'll tell Miss Edith and she'll tell Harriet what she needs to know. Otherwise, complete silence on this issue. Agreed?"

"Agreed," she responded, understanding the seriousness of the problem.

The whole story was revealed including the part about the large pool of blood, now not even a spot.

All she could muster was, "Wow, you're sure this all happened?"

"Certainly." I showed her the pinch mark on my arm. "The ghost did not approach or communicate with me, but it was an unbelievably intense experience for Robert."

"What do you think Robert will do?"

"Robert admitted he had thought about John's demise, but I hope he was convinced that no good would come of it." Still in my mind was my concern that when Robert was in total control, he could rule over John.

Cinnamon was still concerned. "You're right, Arthur. I watched the two of them grow up. John always had to take a back seat to Robert. Now that you know all this, what are you going to do about it? What happens now?"

I was silent for a moment, then replied, "I'm not sure yet. A walk will do me good."

In the early morning the mist hung in the low spots, making the land look surreal. As I walked through the cotton fields, I felt that I had gone back in time by one hundred and fifty years. How bloody the Civil War must have been. I've always felt I was born a hundred years or so too late. To see the old photos of a country before inter-states, factories, and development made me wish for adventure; but, I knew in my heart that if I had lived during the Civil War I would have been killed. It didn't matter which side I would have fought for.

As I approached the house, reality sank in. This case needed to be wrapped up today. JJ and Sarah Jane were eating when I entered the kitchen. JJ said with his tongue in his cheek, "Arthur, pull up a chair to this finger-licking breakfast. Sarah Jane is at least letting me have sugar free jam."

Sarah Jane was smiling. Clearly, they hadn't heard anything during the night. JJ asked, "Arthur, what happened to Robert? We expected him to stay for breakfast."

Fibbing, I told him that Robert woke up early and decided he wanted to see his son before he went to work. That pleased Sarah Jane.

Starving from ghost haunting and a long walk, the orange juice, steaming hot oatmeal and coffee tasted good to me. JJ's expression said he wasn't happy with his new diet. We ate in silence for a few moments.

"You and Robert straighten out whatever you had in mind?" JJ asked. "I still don't understand why he had to stay the night."

Ken Zahn

"We talked out a lot of issues. You will see some changes." Although vague, this needed to be left on a positive note.

Sarah Jane again looked pleased, the happiest I had seen her. She was an ally. The moment was right.

"Are you ready to proceed with the planning?" Both were startled my directness. While they recovered their composure, Cinnamon came by and poured me a second cup of coffee. She signaled me to slow down.

When JJ didn't say anything, Sarah Jane spoke up. "Arthur, it's like me remodeling this house; JJ has no choice. I'm not going to let JJ go through this operation without a plan in place. I trust you because you have nothing to gain by us doing this plan. JJ and I want you to proceed. What do we do next?"

Fortunately, JJ's attorney and CPA knew my meeting with JJ was this week. Both had said they would make themselves available within reason. The plan had been scanned and sent to the attorney and CPA last night. First there would be individual discussions and then conference calls. This wouldn't be as easy it appears, but I have done it many times.

We finished breakfast. It was still too early to call the attorney. The CPA was in another time zone. JJ motioned me into his room. Sarah Jane stayed in the kitchen to talk with Cinnamon about the day's chores.

"Come on, what happened with Robert? There was a little noise when you went up."

"We threw a lot at him and so he and I talked about it late into the night. I don't know, but I expect there'll be some change in his attitude." His question was never answered, but he seemed satisfied with the word "attitude."

"I sure hope you made some progress. Sarah Jane may not be strong enough to keep the two of them separated if I don't survive." He knew the problem.

"Please promise me that you will concentrate on the planning, not Robert." This was a time for single mindedness. Robert would come later.

He agreed, but still seemed concerned.

At 8:30, JJ called the attorney. He wasn't in yet but would arrive by 9:00. His assistant confirmed the commentary and flow charts had arrived and he would call back as soon as possible. He had it on his calendar.

Why not call the CPA's office? Gale was in. After a brief conversation she confirmed the plan was in her hands as we spoke. I explained that I wanted to start with the attorney first, but I expected her to be heavily involved. She said she was reviewing what I sent. Fortunately, it wasn't tax time or this would be impossible. There was nothing for us to do until the attorney called.

JJ called his office to tell Betty he wasn't coming in. "Arthur, excuse me for a moment. Betty just gave me a call I have to make." I got up and left JJ's room. Sarah Jane joined me in the parlor shortly.

"There is so much history here. I hope Miss Edith will see me and tell me what she knows." It was obvious that she was satisfied with the plan and wanted to move on to something more fun. That was both good and bad.

"Make it simple for her. Go alone. Ask her if you can record her conversation. You won't have to take notes or make her repeat herself, and then everyone can hear later what she said."

"Good idea," she agreed.

Sarah Jane talked to me about her growing-up years, when people still talked about the War Between the States, how cotton was king and how much she had enjoyed living here. "I don't know what I will do if JJ dies." Her eyes overflowed with tears. "My life is built around him. He's like a kid who has never grown up. I'm glad he has his buddies and his land buying deals to keep him out of my hair some of the time, but when I think of life without him, well, it would be just empty."

"It will be OK."

The phone rang, but it wasn't the attorney. Sarah Jane could tell who it was on the phone from hearing JJ's end of the conversation. "I'm going in to cut JJ off. JJ and this old college roommate can carry on for hours."

Sarah Jane passed through the doorway into JJ's study and motioned him to end his chat. She returned as JJ was ending his conversation. "C'mon into JJ's room. We'll sit with him while we wait for our attorney to call. That way, I can be sure JJ stays off the phone." The phone rang again and this time it was the attorney, Len. We went to speakerphone.

Ken Zahn

"Arthur, this is quite a plan. I would never have expected JJ to be willing to execute this complex transaction. What's your timeline on doing this?" Len asked.

"Today." My tone was serious.

He gasped. That wasn't unexpected.

"This would normally take a couple of weeks of research and analysis. Lancaster is a multi-million dollar business," the attorney protested strongly.

There was a pause. "Next hour or two." No letting up on my part. JJ and Sarah Jane were quiet.

The attorney also wasn't going to give up.

"Arthur, you know this falls under Chapter 14 and Section 2701 rules. This is not a simple matter. That's why I need more time."

JJ and Sara Jane just listened. This was technical banter. There was no hesitation on my part as the conversation continued. "Section 2701 really applies to noncumulative preferred stock. The preferred will bear an annual cumulative dividend. Second, instead of gifting all the common to family members, a little will be retained by JJ and 10 percent will be gifted to the University. That is an unusual approach in recapitalizations."

He took a deep breath. He was trying to stay ahead of me, but before he could reply, I continued my train of thought. "The University will want a fair gift value so they can redeem the stock eventually. The gift value will set the income tax deduction for JJ. All of this will fix the value of the preferred and the remaining common shares. Remember, we have a $8 million gift tax exemption available for at least the next year or so. JJ is willing to pay gift taxes if necessary." JJ glared at me, but he knew I was forcing the attorney's hand. He actually smiled.

The lawyer began to sputter a bit. "Well, OK but...." Then Sarah Jane spoke up. She sensed Len's reluctance. "JJ needs a serious operation. We're trying to schedule it as quickly as possible. This planning has to be done and done right now." Sarah Jane's tone gave Len very little leeway. Just as it was for Robert, this was uncertain ground for Len. JJ was quiet. I was just a planner in the eyes of the attorney. They were his clients.

After a moment of silence and to buy Len some time, I spoke up. "You can start by doing some preliminary analysis just to see if there are any rulings or tax laws that would collapse the plan." Sarah Jane smiled at me because she knew Len needed to do this right.

He then switched to a different issue. "What about the uncertainty of the qualified dividend rule?"

"The qualified dividend rule is the icing on the cake. If we could freeze the assets in the estate and create a gift to the University to reduce the value of the remaining common shares, we would significantly reduce estate taxes at both JJ's and Sarah Jane's deaths. The estate tax considerations far out-weigh income tax considerations. My estimate of estate taxes before and after the planning is on the last page."

"That much?" Interesting, that's what JJ said.

"Yep, estate taxes aren't going to go away. If the current exemption stays in effect, or close to it, the taxes could eat away a third of the estate at the second death without any planning."

Len agreed that the figures didn't lie. Because he wanted to help JJ, he asked for a few hours for reviewing the law and consulting with other attorneys. That was a very fair response. I gave a thumbs up to Sarah Jane and JJ.

No stopping me now. With no major negatives from the attorney, the next call was to the CPA. Gale had already had an hour to review the plan again. She agreed that this was a good plan when I pointed out that this would also reduce the retained earnings of the company. She too was worried about Chapter 14 and the qualified dividend rule. We went back and forth on that. Fortunately when something gets repeated in different ways, it becomes easier to understand. JJ and Sarah Jane were starting to understand the legal and tax issues.

"Does JJ see you are going to spend some of his money to fight the IRS on the common stock valuations?" Gale had a laughing fit and JJ rolled his eyes, but the tension was broken. She was in rare form.

"Maybe the University would want the value to be high because of the redemption stock feature and would probably spend their money to fight the IRS on valuation. Then JJ and Sarah Jane would get a larger charitable deduction, a new wing on a University building in their name and some 50 yard line seats. This would cut the value of the preferred stock and increase the value of the common stock that would be gifted to their sons." JJ had his thumb up, smiling.

There was silence while Gale thought. The plan could be defeated by JJ's advisers. They had the final say.

"JJ, you do understand that it still could cost you $1 million to fight the IRS? But it will save 50 percent in total taxes." JJ rolled his eyes. Gale had a smile in her voice. Sarah Jane was holding JJ's hand again.

It was Gale, not the attorney, who would probably be battling the IRS. "Please look for any major problems. Once Len is ready, we'll set up a conference call."

Before hanging up, she said, "Arthur, does Len have any major objections?"

"He said he needs more time. There are only two issues, the preferred stock recapitalization and the gift of the company stock to the University. This is not simple planning. He's worried he will miss something. I understand."

After hanging up, we all looked at each other. "This will be a long day of waiting. If the attorney doesn't call by 11:30, he won't call until after lunch. We might as well plan a pleasant lunch."

Sarah Jane left to confer with Cinnamon about lunch and then run a few quick errands. "Won't be long."

We sat there, quietly looking out the window. "JJ, have you talked to Robert?" He said, "No. I told my office that I wasn't to be bothered unless it was an emergency."

The only emergency I was worried about was the situation with Robert. The news vacuum was getting me nervous. The waiting was driving me nuts. Things need to happen, bam, bam, bam. JJ was about to get up. Was food on his mind? "JJ, is UGA going to win the SEC championship this year?" Like it or not, I got a team by team earful until lunch, with JJ relishing every word.

When Sarah Jane came back from town, lunch was ready. It was shrimp salad with peaches and Diet Coke. All three of us were quiet.

No one showed up unexpectedly for lunch. To lighten the mood, I asked JJ and Sarah Jane how they met and decided to marry.

First, Sarah Jane offered her version. She said she noticed him at a high school football game. He was playing guard position. She asked around to find out who he was. She went to another local high school. She would later see him in the student union at the University. She found out who his buddies were and got acquainted with them. Before long, she was invited to a house party at the Kappa Alpha fraternity house. He was with a date when they were introduced, but that didn't discourage her. She discovered what classes he was taking and managed to hang around the building when class got out.

"I don't know how many times I got close to him before he noticed me. He never had a chance after that," she purred.

"That's her story. Little does she know that I did see her." JJ laughed. "I just acted like I was in a hurry and blew by her. I couldn't figure out how she was always outside the building the class was in. I knew she was after me, so I played along."

"I don't believe that story." She reached over and squeezed his hand. "He was too involved with his buddies while coming out of class to see me."

He laughed. It was a happy marriage, a long time love affair.

At 1 p.m., the phone rang. JJ went into the study and picked up the phone. He talked briefly and called for us. Sarah Jane followed me into the study. "It's Len. He'd like to speak to you privately."

The lawyer wasted no time on pleasantries. "You're asking a lot with this plan. We don't do recaps and charitable stock bailouts every day. In fact, you caught everyone at the firm off guard with the plan. We need a lot more time." He sounded annoyed and maybe worried.

"We don't have time. JJ needs serious surgery. We have a matter of days."

"We don't work that way. I don't feel comfortable moving forward with this plan until other planning options have been considered and offered and that will require quite a bit of work on our part. You are talking about drafting Amended Articles of Incorporation, Stockholder Agreement, and issuing new stock certificates. The Amended Articles must be filed with the Georgia Secretary of State. UGA has a Charitable Stock Purchase agreement with a mandatory redemption option. We will need to coordinate that component with the attorneys at the University planning department. "

"OK, can we make it simple for now? What if we issue the preferred stock and establish a dividend percentage to establish the preferred value. After we establish the value of the preferred stock, then we'll issue non-voting common later. JJ can sign all the documentation before the operation. If he dies, the paperwork will be in place. In any case, if he dies we'll face a long, drawn out battle with the IRS. This plan would give you some flexibility in the valuation, gifting, and estate tax reduction. If he lives, there is an added income tax feature. If this doesn't work, it can be undone, can't it?" I asked.

He agreed reluctantly. I didn't let up. "I'm putting you on speakerphone. Does your phone system allow you to do a conference call?"

"Yes, why?"

"I want to get JJ's CPA involved and let her give us her opinion."

"I guess." Now he knew JJ and Sarah Jane would be listening but JJ had been listening on the kitchen phone. Money and JJ were linked.

Soon we were all on the line. The CPA was enthusiastic. With this estate plan saving a high percentage of estate tax and income tax, she felt she could keep the IRS off guard. If the IRS made them pay more estate taxes, then the family would get a bigger step-up in basis and a larger charitable deduction. The University's attorneys would also jump in.

I suspect the attorney was caught off guard by her enthusiasm.

"I can bushwhack them." There was a professional smile in Gale's voice. Wow, what a statement.

Sarah Jane spoke up, her voice firm.

"I want it done so we can concentrate on JJ's health. I don't hear any major negatives. Right now, we're at the mercy of the IRS."

JJ was silent. Sarah Jane had taken over. After a pause the attorney said, "I'll prepare the basic paperwork and overnight it to you in a day or two at most. I need it signed and returned before JJ goes in for surgery. However, I will need you to sign an engagement letter that I will enclose with the documents. I also will enclose a document which will waive liability associated with the tax result from the plan as well as any other overall consequences of the plan. Professional liability will be limited to the compliance of the documents and their filing applicable to state and federal law."

JJ, who had been silent, spoke up. "I understand and I want to proceed." This legal discussion had dampened our mood somewhat. There were some quiet goodbyes. Everyone hung up.

"I'm sorry I was so abrupt, but it's as if someone was planning my funeral. I felt dead already, hearing the way you all talked about me."

Sarah Jane excused herself and left. JJ wasn't finished with me. "Arthur, I have a feeling Len put you on the hook if the plan doesn't work. I heard the whole conversation."

"Yep, but I have been there before. Frankly, Len wasn't himself. He was probably informed by the attorney firm to make those statements. I pressured Len to 'fish or cut bait' and his firm may not have liked it. You must understand, this plan was very close to a tax and legal document and I am not a tax attorney."

"From what I heard, his firm and UGA know how to do this. Why didn't anyone speak up? I am not worried about whether the documents will work with Georgia or the University. I have enough influence with my friends to make Georgia secede from the Union." We both laughed. Color came back into his face.

JJ needed to get out of the house, go to the office, or go visit a friend. When I told him that, he nodded in agreement. Maybe he'd go to the office to see what was happening with Robert. He left without saying where he was headed.

Sarah Jane was still in the kitchen. "I'm going to see Miss Edith to say goodbye," I said to her.

"Oh, Arthur, could I go with you?" she asked.

"No, but I will arrange for you to visit her at some other time."

Actually, the Sheriff was first on my list. Cinnamon called Harriet for a meeting with Miss Edith in about an hour.

CHAPTER SEVENTEEN

There was no traffic in town and there were only a few cars parked on the main street. Was it always so quiet in town? Maybe it was different on weekends. JJ had to step in and help this town. There was no one parked in front of the Sheriff's office.

Upon entering the office, Nancy just waved me back. Crime must be at a minimum in this area. The Sheriff was in his office. Unlike Nancy's desk, his desk was clear of all paper. There were a few certificates on the office wall and some miscellaneous personal pictures. He looked pleased to see me.

"C'mon in and sit down. This has to be the deadest day during my term of office." He realized what he had said and grinned.

Managing a laugh, I replied, "No one died that I know of yet." He didn't know if he should laugh.

"How are you doing with Robert?" He got down to business quickly.

"Don't know for sure. One way or another I'm leaving in the morning. It's too late in the day to leave today." That was actually another fib. I had to sleep in the bed tonight.

He walked around his desk and sat down next to me. "Anything I can help you with? I'm still worried about Robert."

"Don't think so. I just wanted to come by and tell you that I appreciate the help you gave me." That was an understatement. He led me to Miss Edith and saved me from Robert.

"Will I ever find out what happened last night? "

"Not unless you need to know. But I'll call you in the morning. By then I'll know if you should worry or not." I really didn't know what else to say.

"Fair enough. Are you going to see Miss Edith again?"

"Yes."

"Can you ask if she'll see me?"

"Yes, I'll make arrangements with Harriet and she will call you."

Everyone wanted to see this lady. I needed to see an old picture of her! I thanked the Sheriff again as he walked me to the door. He looked outside. "All clear, Arthur," he laughed out loud. I think he was happy he had gotten involved with me, even though it was in a minor way.

As I started to walk out, Nancy got up and hugged me. Wow, somehow I had been able to pull them together. My visit would be a topic of conversation for years to come.

Approaching Miss Edith's house, I could see no cars or people. The town was devoid of life even though it was a work day. Even Harriet smiled as she opened the front door.

"Miss Edith is looking forward to seeing you. Two glasses of sweet tea?"

"Why not?"

Miss Edith had just gotten up from her nap. She was dressed in her Sunday best. "Arthur, come in. I can't begin to tell you how happy I am to see you. The excitement you've brought to this old lady, why you've revved me up. I was feeling sorry for myself. Now sit down and tell me everything that's happened."

Ken Zahn

Before I began, I waited for Harriet to bring my tea and leave the sitting room. "Miss Edith, you have some admirers that want to visit you. May I say they can call?"

"Who?" She gave me a quizzical glance.

"Sarah Jane and the Sheriff."

She said nothing while she considered these two visitors. I added, "Maybe Robert."

I replayed the past night for her. It took her breath away. "He's aware that you know what's going on. You're the only person he can talk to besides me. Would you see him?" I asked.

"Would he tell me what he saw? He saw the murder, didn't he?"

"Yes."

Blinking back tears, she looked out the front window. "I've been thinking about my grandmother. I think she would be proud of me."

"I'm sure of that. Without you taking me into your confidence, there would probably be another tragedy in that house. You made sense of what was going on there for me. Miss Edith, I'm grateful to you."

She gave me a warm smile and after a moment of silence asked, "What happens next?"

"I don't know. It's up to Robert."

"What are you going to do Arthur, if this doesn't work?"

"I'm sleeping in the bed tonight. I haven't slept well for three nights and it's a long drive to Tampa."

"Are you afraid of the bed?"

"You know, Miss Edith, the ghost didn't seem to bother me last night. The ghost delivered his message to Robert. I've done my job. There will be no appearance tonight."

"You sure? Will you call me before you leave tomorrow? It would make me satisfied."

"Of course. Can I tell Sarah Jane and the Sheriff you will see them?" I replied.

"Yes." she sighed

I am gutsy so I asked if she had any old pictures of herself. "No," she lied. My office would search high and low for a photograph. We said goodbyes and I reminded her to let Harriet know she'd be having some visitors. "Arthur, getting to know you has been absolutely marvelous. Y'all come back now, you hear?" Harriet waved to me from the kitchen as I left.

Heading back to the Lancaster home, I thought about Miss Edith. Her looks may have faded but she still had spirit and spunk. I hoped she decided to get out more. She had so much to contribute to the town. Maybe she could bring a spark of pride back to the place.

Entering the house, I discovered that JJ and Sarah Jane were gone. The house was quiet and there was no sign of Cinnamon. I sat down in the parlor. The ticking of the grandfather clock in the corner was mesmerizing and I must have nodded off. The back door slammed and I heard JJ as he came down the hall and into the parlor.

He looked happy. Maybe he had good news. I let him talk first. "Arthur, I had a good afternoon. Met with one of my buddies, had pecan pie with ice cream and sweet tea."

Yipes! I thought to myself. He went on. "Thought what the hell, might as well go out enjoying myself. Don't tell Sarah Jane." He gave me a guilty grin like a little boy has when his parents catch him with his hand in the cookie jar. He rambled on and on about a possible new land deal his buddy had told him about. He was on a sugar rush and feeling no pain. This wasn't what I wanted to hear.

Eventually he said, "I went in the office. Everyone was extremely quiet and working hard. Worried me some."

He was dragging this out. He knew something but he wanted me to ask about it. No way. I kept my mouth shut.

"There's a change. I could feel it when I was there. John was already making arrangements for Robert to handle more of his affairs. Robert was listening and paying attention, rather than telling John he was doing it the wrong way."

"When I went to my office, Betty said she was happy I was going to have my operation. She said she had noticed I had not been feeling well." I was stunned. "Come to find out the boys had made a joint announcement about John becoming the VP of Marketing and Robert the VP of Operations. Then they blabbed about my operation and then said they would be running the company during my recovery."

Ken Zahn

"I'm impressed." Amazed was more the response.

"Wait until I tell Sarah Jane. This is going to cost me some money to do this outside marketing position, isn't it?" JJ kept a tight hold on the purse strings.

"Yes, but if John does a good job, it will lead to more business. If he and Robert work together, you'll get better prices for crops and have a more efficient operation."

"I thought so. Did you just make this up?"

I didn't answer. Let him keep on guessing. I had this sheepish grin on my face.

"I suspected as much. Getting Cindy out of Sarah Jane's way is worth it. The less Sarah Jane has to see Cindy, the better."

"It's not as important to get Cindy out of Sarah Jane's way as it is to get her out of Robert's way," I said.

"Damn, you see everything. I don't know how many times I saw Cindy brush up against Robert. I don't think he has a thing for her anymore but one never knows."

"Maybe a couple of children would change Cindy in many ways."

He laughed, and rolled his eyes skyward.

"Sarah Jane liked that idea. I hope Cindy comes around to wanting a family."

"JJ, if you start giving stock to Bobby, Cindy will change her attitude. In addition, she'll be around her friends with their kids."

"I hope you are right."

When Sarah Jane returned, JJ spent quite a bit of time talking to her about John and Robert working together. They were upbeat and positive. What a change from the first night when Sarah Jane cried.

I excused myself and went up to my room. Might as well pack up before dinner, since I had nothing else to do. I wanted to get an early start in the morning. The late afternoon sun warmed the room. It was so peaceful that I almost sat down in the easy chair to rest for awhile. Resisting temptation, I started packing and even called Silvia to tell her I would be back by late afternoon. She wanted to question me, but I said it was too long a story. I said I was going to write a book about it. She laughed and hung up. Then I went downstairs.

The Parlor

Dinner was superb. Cinnamon went all out. Sarah Jane and JJ were charming. It was clear that they were very happy. Both of them seemed relieved. They were rebuilding their family and business. No matter what happened next, they seemed prepared.

The night was ending in the parlor where it all started. Even two cups of coffee left me sleepy. "It's been a busy few days. If you don't mind, I'm going to turn in." Of course, I wasn't about to tell them how busy my nights there had been.

CHAPTER EIGHTEEN

After finishing my packing, I turned off the lights and sat down by the window, hoping to look at the stars. No such luck. A weather front was moving in. Lightning flashed on the horizon.

The storm brought gusts that made the house creak. Hard rain began to fall. The rain was steady, not like the Florida gully washers. It lasted awhile. The room turned damp and cold. It was bed time so I changed and buried myself and my anxiety under the covers.

For a long time, I listened to the rain on the windows. The sounds of the storm acted like a natural sleeping pill. Dead tired, I fell into a deep sleep, lulled by the rain on the window. The light of the sun woke me. I shivered because cold gripped the room. My first thought was to check the pillow. No blood spot! No ghost! Interesting, but not enough to satisfy me.

I showered and dressed quickly, ready to head home. I hadn't brought any warm clothes, so I put on as many layers as possible. The temperature difference between Georgia and Florida could be extreme. The car heater would be on when I left and the air conditioning on when I arrived in Tampa. Outside, everything was squeaky clean. The plants glistened; the clay was a damp dark red and the air crystal clear. When I heard noise downstairs, I headed for breakfast.

Cinnamon was busy preparing breakfast. JJ was up. Good, we'd have a chance to talk alone. We had our first cup of coffee. For the first time since I arrived, I felt rested.

"Arthur, that was a great rain last night. We got a couple of inches over five to six hours. Couldn't ask for more. What are your plans? When are you leaving?"

"After I check with your attorney and CPA to see if I need to do anything else today, I will be leaving," I looked at the wall clock.

We shared thoughts about being a farmer, living in a small town, and, of course, about Georgia football. Sarah Jane came in, gently telling him to shut up.

After looking outside at the foliage, Sarah Jane talked about yesterday afternoon. Apparently, she and Susan had toured the town and decided to work together on a beautification project. Their first project was new plantings by the old monument in town.

"JJ, I am going to spend some more of your money." He choked on his piece of toast. I spoke up, "I am willing to give one day of my fee to Sarah Jane for this project, but I expect Lancaster to match."

"No, Lancaster will triple after we double your fee." Sarah Jane just glared at JJ.

I said, "JJ, you have to help this town. I will send you a list of ideas that other small towns have used to attract tourists. That would create jobs and a reason for young people to stay here."

"Arthur, you really are a peculiar person. I would have never expected town growth and beautification to be on your financial planning list." Then in a very somber tone he said, "Before you came I was very depressed and really didn't care if I lived, but now I am ready to have that operation. I want to see how this all turns out." He actually cried.

After a leisurely breakfast, I made my calls on JJ's downstairs phone. The attorney indicated that it would be another day before he could send anything. More time was needed, but there were no

Ken Zahn

arguments on his part. The CPA was just as excited as yesterday. I told her we would be working together tomorrow. She had already prepared preliminary calculations.

Since we could work by e-mail, fax and phone, there was no reason to stay around. Nothing more to say. I brought my belongings downstairs.

Sarah Jane pulled me aside. "Arthur, about Miss Edith."

"Call her. She's expecting it."

"Will you wait while I phone?"

"Sure."

Sarah Jane dialed the number. I heard Harriet yelling that tomorrow after Miss Edith's nap would be a good time, about 3 o'clock. She asked, "Is Arthur there?" Sarah Jane replied that I was.

"Harriet says Miss Edith wants to say goodbye."

I had planned to call Miss Edith either on my cell phone or from my office, but I took the phone.

"Robert is here. And I hope to see you again," said Miss Edith quietly.

That message was my Nobel Peace Prize. Saying goodbye to Miss Edith, I hung up the phone.

Sarah Jane said, "Gee, that was fast."

"I told you Arthur was fast," JJ replied.

I went into the kitchen to say goodbye to Cinnamon.

"Cinnamon, thank you so much for all your help. I am grateful to you." I dropped my voice and told her that there had been no visit from the ghost and no blood spot on the pillow last night. She gave me a dazzling smile.

"Arthur, I will miss all the excitement you created during the last four days."

JJ and Sarah Jane were waiting for me by the front door. They walked out with me and waited while I stowed my bags. I'm not a sentimental guy but I was touched by seeing them standing there holding hands. Sarah Jane was teary and gave me a big hug.

"Oh, Arthur, I had no idea when JJ told me you were coming that you would help us so much. Thank you. Thank you."

JJ was biting his lip. He gave me a firm handshake and a slap on the back. "You are something else, Arthur. Worth every penny."

"High praise coming from you, JJ. Thank you. We'll be talking over the next few days. Do me a favor and take care of yourself, OK?"

"You come on back after my successful operation and recovery. We will sit on the 50 yard line and watch Georgia beat Florida."

They both laughed. I got in my car and I headed home. South of town, I called the Sheriff on my cell phone. Nancy answered. The Sheriff was out. Then she said, "Arthur, have you left the Lancaster house?"

"Yes, why?"

"You'll know soon why." She laughed.

On the other side of the hill was the Sheriff's car. He had to know how it ended.